STUBBORN LAWYER (A CANADIAN MYSTERY)

By Donald W. Desaulniers

STUBBORN LAWYER (A CANADIAN MYSTERY)

Copyright 2021, Donald W. Desaulniers

PAPERBACK ISBN: 978-1-989683-19-4

TABLE OF CONTENTS

CHAPTER 1 (Little Rebel)

I'm still at age thirty-one every bit as stubborn as I am independent.

For as long as I can remember, I've always fought authority and loathed being told what to do.

My father was in the Canadian military and tried to run our home like a well-oiled airborne division with him in total command.

Fortunately my mother had a lot of spunk and was able to stand up to my father most of the time.

I guess I learned my rebellious ways from Mom.

My two older twin brothers bore the brunt of my father's discipline.

I was born ten years later and was regularly reminded by both my brothers and by my father than I was an unwanted brat. Mom was more diplomatic and merely admitted that I hadn't been planned.

Bobby and Donny were forced to call our father "sir" at all times. Dad believed that doing so was a sign of respect.

I absolutely refused to do so.

My earliest memories involve getting spanked by my father for the unpardonable sin of calling him "Dad" or "Father" instead of "sir."

Despite the physical punishment, I stood my ground much to the delight of my brothers who were able to live vicariously through my resistance.

By the time I was in Second Grade, I had learned not to cry when Dad was doling out punishment for my various crimes.

That resolve likely resulted in more severe spankings but making my point was more important to me.

Both Bobby and Donny left our home in late June of 1999 as soon as they finished high school. I had turned ten years old in April of that year.

At that time we were living at an air force base in Comox,

British Columbia. My brothers both moved to Alberta. I've only seen them once since then and that was at my mother's funeral in 2011.

I was at law school in London, Ontario at the time. Mom and Dad were still living in British Columbia but by then Dad had retired from the military and resided with Mom in Kelowna.

Dad met a much younger woman a few months later and married her just six months after Mom's death. Fortunately they got hitched at city hall in Kelowna. None of our family was invited which spared my brothers and me from having to decline.

Dad died a year later and left his estate to his young bride. It's unlikely that Bobby, Donny or I would have appreciated receiving an inheritance from Dad anyway. He had been too stern a disciplinarian to be a loving father.

I'm getting ahead of myself.

You need to appreciate my main personality trait in order to understand what makes me tick.

My refusal to bend to authority was the driving force behind the complex human being officially known as Jimmy Corbett.

One quirk about our family was that we boys were named Bobby, Donny and Jimmy. Those were our legal birth names rather than Robert, Donald and James.

As a result, I've always answered to Jimmy and no one has ever shortened my name to Jim.

A huge part of my persona involved a smart mouth. I loved sarcasm.

In order to prevent getting my butt kicked by the victims of my saucy comments, I enlisted Dad to teach me the art of self-defence when I was only eleven. That was the single time I actually bonded with my father and I suspect that he was an eager participant because it gave him an opportunity to knock me on my ass over and over again without fear of reprisals from the child welfare folks.

My school marks were excellent in public school even though I was regularly sent to the principal's office as punishment for rude comments I made either to the teachers or to my fellow students.

The crowning achievement of my youthful rebellion occurred in Tenth Grade.

One of my classes was called Art Appreciation and the teacher, an older gentleman named Mr. Baxter decided that the class should conduct an art exhibition in our high school gymnasium the following Saturday morning which was just a week before the Christmas break.

Since none of us had any real talent, Baxter had us pick our individual assignments from a list on the blackboard. To make the selection as fair as possible, Baxter put twenty numbers on bits of paper in a hat and had us pick out a number randomly.

Baxter overheard me make a caustic comment to the students near me.

"That's quite enough of your smart mouth, Corbett. As punishment for your insolence, you can trade whichever number you select with the unlucky student who picks number twenty."

That change of order did hurt me. I picked number seven which would have left quite a few interesting artistic choices for me but I had to trade with Jennifer Wattam who had pulled out the dreaded final number twenty.

The one and only selection left when it finally got around to me was "PHOTOGRAPHY."

"This is great," I gushed in a phony high-pitched voice. "Thanks, Baxter. You've just given me permission to take pictures of nude young girls. The school board will sack you for contributing to the delinquency of a minor."

My classmates laughed but that only made Baxter angry.

"Sorry to disappoint you, Corbett. No photographs of people are permitted. You'll have to take pictures of wildlife or inanimate objects. If I see one solitary photo of a person in your exhibit, nude or otherwise, I'll hit you with a failing grade."

That shut me up but also entrenched my resolve to make Baxter rue the day he decided to enter into a battle of wills with Jimmy Corbett.

I wracked my brain for inspiration and actually took several pictures of various items and scenery using the camera the school had loaned me but I hated the photos. I had no eye for beauty and definitely no artistic talent.

The perfect solution hit me while I was in the bathroom wiping my ass after a bowel movement.

I was just about to toss the used toilet paper in the bowl when I spotted two perfectly round balls of shit floating in the water.

I put the used toilet paper on the floor, pulled up my pants and went into my bedroom to fetch the camera. Then I adjusted the bathroom light a bit and took the first photograph for my art project.

I walked to Wal-Mart and enlarged the photo while inserting the caption "IDENTICAL TWINS" in large letters at the top of the photograph.

The next day I examined another one of my bowel movements. This one also involved two equally-sized turds but one of them had sunk to the bottom of the bowl while the other remained on the surface.

I enlarged this beauty as well at Wal-Mart and added the caption "SINK OR SWIM" at the top.

Baxter had indicated that my exhibit had to include three photographs and I felt that I needed to make the last one special.

A fantastic idea popped into my head and I proceeded to throw in every morsel of my budding artistic talent into the final masterpiece.

Saturday rolled around and I walked to the school with my exhibits carefully covered so that no one could see my photographs until the great unveiling in front of the judges and onlookers.

The art show was arranged in order of the numbers we had picked in class which meant that my own project would be the very last to be viewed and judged.

I had inserted the three photographs in picture frames and hung them up on the wall at the far end of the gym, still covered from prying eyes.

The judges and audience slowly moved from exhibit to exhibit while each student stood beside their creations as each one was unwrapped or uncovered.

When the crowd finally arrived at my station, I waited until all the stragglers had assembled.

"My assigned art project was photography," I explained. "I've attempted to demonstrate how inanimate objects can represent certain complex concepts. The first photo questions the theory that each one of us is unique. The second picture tackles the idea of education and the harsh lesson that not all of us are destined to succeed. The final photograph juxtaposes the joy of socialization with the incontrovertible fact that folks can have totally different tastes and preference. I hope you enjoy my creation and that it makes you ponder deeply about the concepts shown therein."

With that artsy preamble, I yanked the sheet off the three photographs.

The reaction from the four judges, each of whom was a teacher at the school, ranged from mild amusement to utter disgust.

The spectators, most of whom were other students, broke into raucous laughter mixed with comments about how gross the exhibit was.

My third photograph was indeed a work of art.

It consisted of a rather large light brown turd on which I had carefully placed several kernels of corn, a few green peas and a juicy red strawberry.

The caption at the top of the picture announced "LET'S DO LUNCH."

Sadly I didn't win a ribbon or even an honorable mention for my exhibit but Old Man Baxter gave me a "B+" which meant that I didn't flunk that course.

I describe that day in lurid detail to you now because in my mind it best represented my rebellious and independent nature.

CHAPTER 2 (A Welcome Escape)

That little rebel eventually transformed into a somewhat difficult adult.

I finished high school and then attended university first in Waterloo followed by law school in London, Ontario.

My marks were excellent and I won various scholarships but when I'd finally finished law school, my belligerent attitude turned off practically every recruiter who interviewed me.

The end result was that the only choice left to me was to take my articles with a mid-sized Toronto law firm famous for obscenely overworking its staff.

My life devolved into what I considered to be white slavery consisting of eighty hour work weeks.

When my articles were completed, the firm offered me a position as a junior attorney at a healthy starting salary of $140,000 per year provided that I met my billing targets.

I've stuck it out here for almost seven years in order to obtain good litigation experience and also to allow me to pay off my debts and save up some money.

Unfortunately I never enjoyed the job. The hours I needed to toil in order to meet my billing targets were bad enough, but the actual legal work was unfulfilling. Most of my files were matrimonial litigation which was a soul-destroying way to earn a living.

I was forced to listen to a wide range of marital woes after which my job was to suck as much money as possible out of my client's ex-spouse while at the same time maximizing my legal fee.

I've had no social life but thankfully hadn't turned into a lush like so many of my colleagues.

My rebellious temperament was generally kept in check and only twice had I butted heads with the partners.

In both of those cases the partners instructed me to fight about issues that were sure losers and I stubbornly refused to do so. They gave in and I'm pleased to report that on both files my clients obtained a much superior result than they would have if we had stirred the pot by making claims that had no realistic chance of success.

Working like a slave was a tremendously effective antidote to rebellion. Besides, it wasn't my law firm. I was merely an employee so generally toed the line and didn't purposely offend my fellow attorneys, none of whom were personal friends.

With no social life to spend my money on, I invested most of my wages.

As soon as I was hired on as an attorney after completing my articles and bar admission course, I purchased a small home within easy walking distance of the office. The vendor was an estate and the furniture was included in the purchase price which saved me the cost and time required to buy my own furniture.

My old car died three years ago and I never replaced it. My home was near a bus stop and I had rarely used my car after I began articling.

Last winter the American stock market had tanked and a couple of the lawyers at the law firm had persuaded me to invest some money in American stocks while their value was remarkably low. That advice had so far been stellar and I had already earned at least fifty percent in pure profit.

Although my financial picture was rosy, the Covid-19 shutdowns and other restrictions had made 2020 a terrible year for me and for almost everyone else.

It was now one week before Christmas and Ontario was shut down again. The court system had been appallingly inefficient since March although that fact had made it somewhat easier to reach mutual settlements.

No spouse wanted to wait months or even longer for a simple motion to be heard by a judge.

Today was Thursday, the 17th of December, 2020.

The receptionist poked her head in my office at three o'clock.

"Jimmy, there's a special meeting of all the lawyers in the firm beginning at four o'clock in the main conference room. Attendance is mandatory."

"Thanks for the warning, Holly."

I wondered what the meeting was about. Perhaps the firm was going to dole out the annual bonuses a week early this year.

Just before four o'clock I shut off my computer and headed for the conference room.

This firm consisted of thirty attorneys of whom twelve were partners, seven were associates like me and the remaining eleven were lowly junior lawyers. The firm hadn't hired any articling students this year.

Howard Goose, the managing partner called the meeting to order at five minutes past four.

"This pandemic has badly affected the firm's bottom line this year. The partners had hoped to ride out the lockdowns but there's no sign now that they're going to be ending any time soon. That unfortunately means that we've got to trim some costs in order to maintain our optimum profitability."

I let out a loud groan. The other zombies were as silent as statues.

Goose continued.

"No Christmas bonuses will be paid this year. In addition there will be two associate and four junior positions terminated immediately. The partners have discussed which of you might be affected but we haven't come to final decisions. We have decided to give those terminated the required legal notice rather than severance pay in lieu of notice."

This time several attorneys either groaned or gasped.

It was so typical of this slimy law firm. In my own case, I'd be entitled to roughly six months' notice or severance. The firm could fire me but force me to work until next July when the termination would become effective.

Goose had more to say.

"If any associates or junior attorneys volunteer to leave the employ of this firm, then we are willing to pay one-half of the minimum required severance and not require that lawyer to work through the notice period. If that option might interest you, please raise your hand now."

My hand immediately shot up.

No one else volunteered.

"Thank you, Jimmy. Is anyone else interested in a similar arrangement?"

Everyone looked down at the floor.

"In that case, this meeting is over. Jimmy, please follow me to my office."

I walked along with Mr. Goose.

"We'll be sorry to see you leave, Jimmy. Your antics have provided us with great entertainment over the years and your work has always been excellent. What do you think you'll do with your life now?"

"I haven't had a chance to think about it, Howard. I thrust my hand in the air because I saw your offer as a chance to escape the rat race."

"I hope you don't regret your decision, Jimmy."

We sat in his office while Goose examined my compensation package. I currently earned $302,000 per annum. Half of the six month severance worked out to slightly more than $75,000.

We came to an agreement that I would work at the firm until January 5th and that the severance would be paid to me in 2021 rather than this month.

Goose was pleased with the arrangement because it gave me three weeks to finalize most of my files or at least sort them out to the extent that they could be transferred to another lawyer in the firm.

I was also satisfied.

My prison sentence was almost over.

CHAPTER 3 (Unusual Opportunity)

I quit work at eight o'clock, at least two hours earlier than normal.

That evening I decided to sell my home and leave Toronto.

The next morning I contacted a realtor who dropped by at lunch time to see my home. Apparently the real estate market was hot despite the time of year and I listed the place for an astounding $1,450,000 which was more than half a million bucks higher than I had originally paid for the house.

Several offers were delivered to me on Wednesday, the 23rd of December and I accepted one with a closing date of January 7th. The price was $50,000 above asking which excess covered the flat realty commission I had negotiated with the agent.

For the ensuing two weeks I worked reasonably long hours

because I wanted to close out as many files as I could.

New Year's Day 2021 arrived and I still had no clue about my future except that I wanted to leave Toronto.

One of my fantasies had been to travel for a few months but the pandemic restrictions made that option untenable.

Another possibility was to open up my own legal practice somewhere in Ontario. That choice had a lot of appeal because I yearned to be my own boss so that I could exert some control over my working hours as well as the type of files I took on.

Deciding where to realize that dream was the immediate obstacle.

I really disliked living in the huge metropolis of Toronto which prompted me now to consider a small town. That's as far as my tentative plan got. I looked at the map of Ontario but couldn't decide where I might like to live.

I actually worked for six hours on New Year's Day and planned on working even longer hours the following day which was Saturday.

Howard Goose had dropped into my office on December 31st in order to check on my progress with closing out my files. He seemed very pleased with what I had accomplished.

"How are you coming along with the Bannon file?" Howard inquired once he had determined that it was still active.

"It's a dog's breakfast, Howard. The opposing attorney is being totally unreasonable and we've had several rather heated arguments. I doubt very much if any progress can be made before my departure."

"As a personal favor to me, would you give that file some immediate attention? Harvey Bannon is one of my best friends and he's become very distraught about the whole marital mess."

"I'll see what I can do but it's very possible that another attorney here in the firm might have more success dealing with opposing counsel."

"The partners and I have always been impressed with your creativity, Jimmy. I can assure you that we wouldn't have terminated you. Please give the Bannon file your best efforts."

I had taken Howard's plea to heart and yesterday I had spent the entire six hours on that one file.

First thing this morning I had set up a meeting at the other lawyer's office for one o'clock. Harvey would accompany me and his spouse would also be present. Saturday meetings were not uncommon. Most attorneys worked on Saturdays.

Harvey called at quarter to one that he was in our firm's parking lot. I went out to meet him and we drove to the other office.

Harvey and I had spoken at length yesterday about softening our demands regarding various financial issues.

The strategy paid off big time because the meeting turned out to be a huge success. The wife appeared to be just as anxious to get the separation details settled and overrode her attorney's advice several times during the two hour meeting.

The agreement was amended immediately to reflect the new terms and both spouses signed the final version in the presence of the other attorney and me.

Harvey was ecstatic as he drove me back to my office.

"Howard says that you're leaving the firm later this week."

"That's right. The pandemic has necessitated a modest downsizing of the firm and I volunteered to be one of the lawyers to get the sack."

"Howard also admitted that they were sorry to lose you. What prompted you to quit the firm?"

"Working at least eighty hours each week is no life worth living."

We discussed my plans. Harvey was shocked that in fact I had made no fixed plans other than to sell my home.

"My great-niece lives in the small city of Belleville about a hundred miles east of Toronto. She and her husband broke up recently and he's being a real bastard. Nicole contacted an attorney last week but didn't feel comfortable with the woman's recommendations. Would you be willing to discuss Nicole's situation with her? I'd look after your legal account."

"That's a possibility. Belleville was one of the cities I was looking at as a potential place to begin the next phase of my life."

"I understand that Tuesday is your final day at Howard's firm."

"That's correct."

"Would you be able to see me on Wednesday morning at my home? We can contact Nicole and run my proposal by her."

"I'll need to purchase a vehicle. I don't own a car right now."

"My son owns a dealership in Pickering. I'll have him call you tonight. You can discuss what sort of vehicle you're interested in and I'll make Henry give you a tremendous deal."

"That sounds great."

We settled on seven o'clock for the phone call. I had no intention of working after six this evening.

When I got back to my apartment at six-thirty, I checked out the city of Belleville on my smart phone. It had a population of 50,000 and the real estate prices seemed very reasonable. There were a lot of lawyers there but Belleville was the county seat.

Henry called precisely at seven o'clock.

"What sort of vehicle are you looking for, Jimmy?"

"I'm not a pretentious guy, Mr. Bannon. My preference would be to purchase an older model car with as few computer gadgets as possible."

"That limits the choice considerably. I operate a Hyundai dealership and we restrict our used inventory to late model vehicles. Yesterday we took in two trades from a chap who purchased a new Santa Fe. One of those vehicles belonged to his late mother. It's a 2003 Chevy Malibu with low mileage. I'd sell it to you for $2,500. That's the only older model I've got in stock. We were going to sell it to a used car dealership which purchases older inventory from us from time to time. It isn't worth our time to market inexpensive older units."

"That sounds perfect for me, Mr. Bannon."

"Dad said that he'd bring you here on Wednesday morning after he picks you up at your apartment. I'll have the car thoroughly checked out for you and we can do the paperwork then."

I thanked Mr. Bannon and was pleased that my business contacts had landed me a set of wheels so effortlessly.

Tuesday was surprisingly busy at the firm.

The unlucky candidates for termination were announced and

that suffused the office with a lot of extra tension.

Howard Goose assigned Darlene Allems to take over my remaining files so I spent the day with her going over each file.

In fact I worked until well after six o'clock. Howard came in to say goodbye and to wish me luck in my future endeavors. He also thanked me profusely for my work on behalf of Harvey. Howard handed me a very effusive letter of recommendation in case I decided to work for another firm and also gave me the check for my severance less the various withholding taxes.

Several other lawyers and secretaries also dropped in over the course of the day to say goodbye.

This place had been my home as well as my prison for more than six years.

I had no regrets about leaving.

CHAPTER 4 (Hello Belleville)

Harvey Bannon showed up as scheduled at nine o'clock on Wednesday morning and drove me to his son's car dealership.

I signed the required documents and paid for my "new" vehicle. It was medium gray in color and had only 75,000 kilometers of mileage despite being old enough to vote assuming the voting age was still eighteen.

While Robert's staff looked after the vehicle transfer, Harvey drove me to his condominium where we phoned his great-niece.

I told Nicole what financial and other information I needed her to round up and we arranged to meet at her apartment on Saturday morning.

Harvey drove me back to Pickering where I picked up my 2003 Chevy Malibu. Later that day I packed my personal belongings into the vehicle. My furniture was included in the sale price of my home because it would have been more expensive to move the items than they were worth.

Since my income for 2021 would almost certainly be far less than I earned in 2020, I decided to sell my stock portfolio and realize the capital gain in this lower earnings year. It only took one phone call to make the arrangements.

My house sale closed without problems on Thursday the 7th and I picked up my certified check for the balance of the sale proceeds that afternoon. I had used one of the real estate attorneys in the law firm and thanked her for making the endeavor painless.

I went to my bank and deposited the net sale funds. After payment of my mortgage, the legal bill and the realty commission, I was still left with $652,300, all of it tax free since principal residences were not subject to capital gains tax.

The sale of my stock portfolio
had netted me another $130,000
although I'd eventually owe about
$12,000 in tax on the capital
gains portion of that sale.

All in all I had a rather
impressive nest-egg with which to
begin my new life in Belleville.

There was no point in remaining
in Toronto tonight so I drove east
and arrived at Belleville shortly
after five o'clock. I found a
hotel and then brought take-out
fast food up to my room for my
supper.

The hotel provided a
complimentary copy of the local
newspaper. After supper I scanned
the paper with special attention
given to apartment rentals.

I also used my smart phone to
search on-line for available
apartments. The pickings were
slim.

While I was on the internet, I
also looked again at home prices
in Belleville.

Two townhouse style waterfront
condominiums looked interesting.

One of them was listed for $579,900 at a complex called The Moorings on the Belleville inner harbor and had its own boat slip but no other amenities.

The other listing was called Pier 31 and a unit on the water was available for $629,900. This condo complex had a swimming pool and tennis court.

On Friday morning I drove past both properties and loved each of them.

While I was at Pier 31 walking around near the pool area, I struck up a conversation with one of the owners.

He mentioned that another unit not overlooking the water had been listed for sale last summer but hadn't sold at the list price of $434,900.

I took a chance and knocked on the door of that unit. The older couple who answered seemed quite interested in selling without having to pay realty commission.

They were pleased to show me the unit which contained three floors of opulent living space plus an unfinished basement. The only feature this unit didn't have was a garage. My two assigned parking spots were outdoors.

I loved the layout and within an hour we had hammered out a tentative agreement whereby I would pay $427,300 with a closing date on the 19th of January. They owned a winterized cottage and would move in there for the time being.

We also arranged that I would buy some of their furniture for an additional $2,700. Doing so would save them having to move many of the larger items including their appliances.

We drove to their lawyer's office where their attorney prepared the purchase agreement. I agreed to employ another lawyer in the same firm to handle my end of things.

Since I had the funds already sitting in my bank account, we moved the closing date up to January 12th which meant that I'd soon be able to move out of the hotel.

Already I was thrilled with my choice of cities. A condo unit like the one I just purchased would cost well over $2,000,000 in Toronto.

CHAPTER 5 (Quick Resolution)

On Saturday morning I drove to Nicole Bannon's high-rise apartment. She buzzed me in.

Nicole had accumulated most of the financial information I had requested.

Her situation was quite typical of younger couples who ended their marriage.

Nicole was twenty-eight and her husband Frank was thirty. They had no children.

Both of them were school teachers although Frank made about $6,000 more than Nicole because he had been working for the school board one year longer.

Frank had already owned the marital home for a year when Nicole moved in six months prior to their marriage which had lasted six years. The title was still registered in just Frank's name.

I examined the finances and list of assets.

The school pensions and the marital home were the main assets.

"This shouldn't be complicated, Nicole. What seems to be the sticking point in the negotiations?"

"Frank won't agree to sell the home and he's claiming that he should be entitled to seventy-five percent of our equity. He says that the home was worth at least $300,000 when we got married. Frank bought it for $202,000 in the late fall of 2013."

"What is the house worth today?"

"Frank says that it's only worth $390,000 but I've looked on the internet and I'm pretty sure it would sell for at least $440,000."

"Where did Frank get his valuation figures?"

"His Deed confirms that he bought it for $202,000 but Frank didn't disclose how he came up with the value at the time we got married or with the current value."

"Have you obtained an appraisal or at least checked the internet to obtain approximate home appreciation values each year since 2013 when Frank purchased the property?"

"No I haven't."

I had Nicole show me a photo of the home. It was a standard back-split model and was built in 1963. Nicole hadn't paid Frank any money to purchase a half interest in the home but they had shared all the house expenses equally from the time they got married.

Frank's mortgage at the time he bought the house was $191,450 and the current balance owing was about $180,000.

The couple had no other debts. They had paid off their own student loans in full and carried no credit card debt.

"Has Frank consulted an attorney?"

"No. He says that lawyers are a waste of money. He wants to pay me $52,500 and have me sign off my spousal interest in the home. We've already divvied up the furniture amicably. Frank also wants each of us to waive any rights to the other's pension."

"You mentioned that you spoke with an attorney. What did she recommend?"

"She wanted to sue Frank for spousal support, half the value of his pension, an equal split of the home equity and occupation rent for the period from when I moved out last month until the matter is finally settled. She also wanted a $5,000 retainer to get started. No offense, but I just didn't trust her."

"Your incomes are near enough to each other that spousal support doesn't appear very viable unless one of your jobs is in jeopardy. The same holds true with the value of your teacher's pensions. His will be worth a bit more than yours because he's worked one extra year but I don't think that's a worthwhile area to fight about."

"Both of us are secure in our positions. We don't teach at the same school."

"Does your pension plan offer free legal representation?"

"No, I didn't opt for that enhancement and neither did Frank."

"Are you contributing to the home expenses now?"

"No. Frank and I agreed that I'd pay my own apartment rent and he'd look after all the house expenses."

"I assume that your rent is actually higher that your previous half share of the house expenses."

"That's correct. It's definitely cheaper to own a home than it is to rent an apartment."

"The equity in the home is really the only area of real contention. Let's see what we can find right now on the internet about local home prices."

We each accessed our smart phones and began searching for the information.

We both came up empty.

"Let's go at it from a different angle," I suggested. "We'll look at current listings."

That angle worked much better.

We found six recently listed homes in town which were roughly similar to Frank and Nicole's house.

The asking price of those homes ranged from $430,000 up to $460,000 and the real estate articles indicated that full price offers were common this month because of high demand. In fact offers higher than the asking price were often received.

"It seems that your estimate of the home's value is more realistic than Frank's. The average of the similar listings is $445,000. If the home was sold, the realty commission would be about $25,000 including the HST. We could pay for a proper appraisal if you were uncomfortable using these average figures."

"I hadn't thought of the real estate commission. I'd be happy to set the home's value at $420,000. That would mean that the equity after paying off the mortgage

would be $240,000. How much of
that should be mine?"

"You were spouses for six out of
the seven years since Frank bought
the place. I can't imagine a judge
not splitting the equity on that
basis. You could fight about how
much the home's value went up in
the one year period before you got
married but if we simply divide
the equity by seven, then each
year the value increased by about
$34,285. Give that sum to Frank
and split the remainder equally.
That would give you $102,857 and
Frank in total would get
$137,143."

"How much would your legal fee
be?"

"Your uncle is willing to pay my
fee. If Frank is amenable to our
offer, then the Separation
Agreement could be prepared with a
minimum of time. I doubt that my
fee would exceed $1,500. Frank
would have to pay a separate
lawyer whatever fee he or she
charged but again, that would be

quite low if the terms of the agreement weren't disputed."

"It was nice of Uncle Harvey to offer to pay your fee but I insist on paying it myself."

"Are you and Frank on speaking terms?"

"Yes."

"You could call him right now and run the proposal by him including how we came up with the figures."

That call went surprisingly well except that Frank was insistent that Nicole's attorney prepare the agreement. All Frank wanted to do was see another lawyer merely to have a witness to his signature and obtain the required certificate of independent legal advice.

Nicole was agreeable.

Since all I had to work with was my smart phone, the logistics of preparing the separation agreement were a bit unusual but in the end I sent a blank standard form to Nicole's desktop computer and prepared the document in her spare bedroom which she was utilizing as her den.

We had to call Frank twice regarding specific wording issues but I got the agreement completed and Nicole emailed it to Frank for his approval.

That resulted in a couple of minor alterations.

Nicole printed off four copies of the final draft and signed them with me acting as witness.

Then Nicole delivered all four signed copies to Frank who would find a lawyer on Monday.

That procedure went without a hitch and by end of business day Nicole had her duly signed two copies. I met her after she finished school.

Nicole paid my account in the amount of $1,243 including tax and provided me with one of her signed copies for my records.

She thanked me profusely for sorting out her affairs. My first and only client as a sole practitioner was now a thing of the past.

CHAPTER 6 (A Temporary Offer)

On Monday morning I had attended at my own lawyer's office and delivered my certified check for the purchase money and lawyer's account.

I had a nice chat with my attorney who seemed quite fascinated with my escape from the rat race and with my tentative plan to establish my own legal practice here in town.

On Tuesday my condo purchase closed late in the day. I had booked my hotel for tonight because the sellers technically had until midnight tonight to vacate the premises.

When I dropped in to my lawyer's office to pick up my keys at the reception desk, the woman buzzed my lawyer to inform her that I had arrived.

Deborah led me down to her office.

"I mentioned your situation to the boss yesterday. If you have a few minutes, he'd like to speak with you."

I was agreeable so Deborah took me to the senior partner whose name was Richard Kaufmann. Deborah introduced us to each other and left.

Kaufmann looked to be in his mid-sixties.

"I understand that you recently left a law firm in Toronto and that you practiced family law litigation."

"That's correct."

"How long had you worked for that law firm?"

"I articled there and then was hired on as soon as I was called to the Ontario legal bar in 2014."

"Why did you leave?"

I explained about the crushing work hours and my spontaneous decision to escape the prison when the firm decided to downsize.

"If you don't mind telling me, how much were you earning at that firm?"

"My salary was about $302,000."

"You'll never earn that much here in Belleville, especially as a sole practitioner."

"That doesn't concern me. I had no social life in Toronto. The job consumed all my time and energies."

Richard asked me a ton of questions about my legal experience.

"You're somewhat overqualified to work in a small town. You won't find many upscale clients like the ones you dealt with in Toronto."

"I believe that I've already had an inkling of that reality. The reason I chose Belleville was that one of my Toronto clients had a relative here who had recently separated and whose spouse was being difficult. In fact their situation was quite uncomplicated and I wrapped up the matter in a single day. I earned my first legal fee as a sole practitioner and now I'm fresh out of clients."

Richard asked me to show him my letter of recommendation which I happened to have with me in my briefcase.

"I'd like to discuss your situation in greater detail, Jimmy. Would you be able to drop in tomorrow morning at ten o'clock to see me?"

I was agreeable and left the office.

The sellers had already fully vacated my new condominium. I was tempted to spend the night in it but decided to remain in the hotel since I'd paid for tonight.

On Wednesday morning I checked out of the hotel and unloaded my belongings into the condo.

I drove to Richard Kaufmann's office and met with him.

"Thanks for taking the time to see me, Jimmy. I took the liberty of speaking with Howard Goose last evening. He speaks very highly of you and admitted that he was sorry to lose you. The reason I invaded your privacy so thoroughly yesterday was that we're in a bind here at the firm and you might be the answer to our prayers."

"I'm not really following you, Richard."

"My specialty is commercial law and I've built up a large business in that area. One of my most influential clients has found herself involved in a dicey family dispute. I took on the file and assigned it to my most competent matrimonial attorney but she found the matter too stressful and has threatened to quit the firm unless I pass the matter along to another lawyer. That's where you come in."

"I'm listening."

"I'd like to hire you on a temporary contract basis to handle mainly that one file. The client has extremely deep pockets and I don't have anyone in the firm who is capable of sorting out the mess. I believed that Belinda was up to the job but it was too much for her."

"How long do you expect that you'd require my services?"

"Three months should be enough time. If you haven't completed the file by then and if you decline to join this law firm, then I'll admit to the client that her problem is beyond our ability to deal with."

"How much will I be paid and what sort of hours would be involved?"

"I'll be charging out your time at $350 an hour but you'll be on salary at either a fixed rate of $15,000 a month or at an hourly rate of $100. In either event you would be expected to work at least thirty-five hours each week."

"I'm virtually certain that I won't be interested in joining your law firm. I really do have a strong desire to operate my own legal practice. Working for you temporarily would give me an opportunity to learn more about Belleville and the legal climate here. Would I be able to look over the client's file before making my decision?"

"I'm afraid not. Confidentiality is paramount. You'd be doing me a great favor by accepting the position. In fact I'm even willing to sweeten the deal. At my sole and total discretion, if you resolve the matter satisfactorily, I'll pay you a bonus which can serve as an incentive to wrap the puppy up."

I accepted the offer.

Suddenly Jimmy Corbett was employed again.

CHAPTER 7 (Getting Started)

We arranged that I'd begin work tomorrow morning at nine o'clock.

Belinda would discuss the file with me in detail and later in the day I would drive to the client's home with Richard Kaufmann in order to meet Beatrice Lantz in person.

I opted for the flat fee of $15,000 per month and promised to spend a minimum of thirty-five hours on the file each week. I roughly calculated that working eighty hours a week for $302,000 annually had earned me about $72 an hour. The old firm had granted its associates two weeks paid vacation each year and I had received a bonus of about $5,000 each Christmas until this past year when the bonus was cancelled.

The reason that I rejected the hourly rate option was that I felt more comfortable not putting myself in a position to be accused of running up the hours without visible results.

I intended to put as many hours as required on resolving the Lantz file. Kaufmann could reflect my extra time in his bonus if he chose to do so. I would keep accurate records of my legal time.

For the remainder of the day I did errands such as buying groceries and beer. The appliances were included in my purchase so I also did laundry.

It felt decadent to be so idle all day.

Indoor dining was still prohibited in Ontario so I cooked my first supper at my new condominium.

On Thursday morning I arrived at the law office shortly after eight-thirty.

Richard introduced me to Belinda Cartright and then left us to discuss the file.

Belinda was several years older than me and seemed well versed in family law.

Her opinion on the various legal issues was very close to my own.

The client had been married for just four years to a chap named Johnathan Jacobs who was fifty-eight years of age. Beatrice Lantz was fifty-seven.

Apparently they had met at a business conference in Toronto and hit it off immediately.

The list of assets of both spouses indicated that Johnathan had very little whereas Beatrice was very wealthy.

No marriage contract had been prepared which meant that the established family law principles and case law applied.

Johnathan was seeking a half share of the increase in value of Beatrice's assets during their marriage. The total increase had been in excess of two million dollars. Johnathan was also seeking spousal support.

The factor which had driven Belinda to the point of quitting the law firm was the unbending attitude of Beatrice Lantz who insisted that Johnathan had substantial cash assets at the time they met. Beatrice was convinced that Johnathan was hiding his wealth although she had no evidence to back up her assertion.

Reading between the lines, it also appeared that there was a personality conflict between Belinda and Beatrice.

Wryly I wondered if my own insanely stubborn streak would clash with Beatrice's firm resolve.

Belinda had avoided all-out war by paying lip service to Beatrice's allegations but advising that without solid evidence there was nothing that Belinda could do.

Beatrice had hired a private detective out of Toronto but he had pretty much come up empty.

Once Belinda had told me all she could about the file, she left it with me and thanked me profusely for taking it off her hands.

I began studying the file.

Richard and I were going to
Beatrice's home at six o'clock
this evening.

CHAPTER 8 (The Stubborn Client)

I left the office at five o'clock and made myself a bowl of soup and a sandwich at my condo after which I returned to the office.

Richard and I took his Cadillac Escalade to Beatrice's home which was what could accurately be described as a mansion on the south side of the Bay of Quinte.

Beatrice was an attractive lady with a no-nonsense attitude and as soon as we had sat down in her living-room, she complained to Richard.

"How can you possibly believe that this young gentleman will be an improvement over Belinda Cartright?"

"Despite Richard's youthful appearance, he was a highly competent family law attorney with a Toronto law firm until last week. I've hired Richard on a temporary contract to focus solely on your legal problem."

"Did you get the sack, Richard?"

"Actually I chose to leave. The firm announced a downsizing shortly before Christmas and asked if anyone wanted to volunteer to quit. I was sick of working eighty hour weeks and raised my hand."

"Why are you now in Belleville?"

"I decided that I wanted to operate my own legal practice in a small town."

I proceeded to explain about my client asking me to help out his great-niece with her marital dispute and that I'd already sorted out that matter and purchased a condo at Pier 31.

"How did you afford a condominium in that upscale complex?"

"I sold my small home in Toronto last week. The prices there are atrociously inflated so I was able to purchase the condo for cash."

"How old are you?"

"I'm thirty-one."

"Are your parents wealthy?"

"My parents died when I was still in law school. I didn't inherit any portion of their estate."

"Why is that?"

Richard kept his mouth shut despite the intensely personal questions Beatrice was peppering me with.

I decided to remain polite.

"My father remarried a younger lady a few months after my Mom passed away and when Dad died the following year he left everything to his new bride."

"Belinda was clearly intimidated by me and that soured me on relying on her legal representation. I can tell already that you're a pushover. You've allowed me to ferret out information about you that I have no business knowing."

"Please don't misinterpret politeness as weakness, Beatrice. My primary attribute is my stubbornness. I can't be intimidated by anyone. My rebellious nature has gotten me in trouble ever since I was a child. I've examined your file in some detail earlier today and Belinda filled me in on her progress to date. Tomorrow I'd like to meet with you and discuss your legal problem fully and frankly. I'll give you my honest opinion."

"What if I don't like your evaluation?"

"I can forewarn you now that you won't like my preliminary opinion. It will be up to you to convince me that your position has merit."

Beatrice was silent for a moment. Richard didn't look happy but he kept his mouth shut.

Finally after a pause of at least a full minute, Beatrice spoke.

"That's fair enough. Bring my file with you. I expect you to arrive promptly at nine o'clock tomorrow morning."

Beatrice stood up to indicate that this meeting was over.

Richard and I said goodnight and drove back to the office.

"Your temporary gig might only last two days," Richard remarked.

"Belinda's evaluation of the legal issues seems to be bang on. Tonight I'll examine Beatrice's file in more detail to make sure I haven't missed some crucial factor, but it seems to me that she is being totally unreasonable in her demands."

"It is what it is. Please try not to offend Beatrice. I'd hate to lose her corporate and commercial business."

"I'll do my best, Richard."

CHAPTER 9 (Unreasonable Claims)

On Friday morning I made breakfast and drove to Beatrice's home.

We adjourned to her study.

"I took your file home with me last evening and studied it quite extensively."

"What were your initial conclusions, Jimmy?"

"It's only been four months since you and Johnathan separated. His attorneys appear to have been candid with their financial disclosures. They even provided Belinda with copies of Johnathan's tax returns and notices of assessment from the tax office for the previous six years along with a rough draft of his anticipated 2020 tax return."

"Are you acquainted with the opposing legal firm?"

"As a matter of fact I have dealt with them a few times during my stint with the Toronto law firm. They do a lot of matrimonial work."

"Did they kick your butt?"

"It's a myth to believe that the party with the better lawyer wins the cases. The facts are the main determinant of the outcome. The two motions you lost are typical."

"What do you mean?"

"The first motion was brought by Johnathan's lawyers to obtain interim spousal support. Belinda shouldn't have contested that motion. The amount of support they requested was reasonable given the disparity in incomes and assets."

"I resented having to pay that disgusting gold digger one red cent."

"I would have tried to persuade you not to fight. The second motion was brought prematurely and that's the reason you lost that motion. I should point out that in both cases you were made to pay the legal account of Johnathan's attorneys."

"Don't remind me. What do you mean by calling the second motion premature?"

"It was based on totally unsubstantiated claims that Johnathan was hiding assets."

"Despite the negative results of that motion, I continue to believe that he has substantial assets of his own."

"The judge ruled that you had no such evidence. The file didn't say whether you and Johnathan attended either of those motions."

"We did not. Both motions were held in judge's chambers and only the attorneys were permitted to attend."

"That's a shame because Belinda's notes are very cursory. I'll ask her later today what actually took place. Let's divide today's interview into two parts. Firstly, we can look at the legal issues. After we've discussed those thoroughly, then we can delve into the issue of Johnathan's buried assets. Does that sound like a reasonable approach?"

Beatrice was agreeable.

"Based on the material in the files, you don't have any realistic chance of success if we take the matter to court. Johnathan's demands are extremely reasonable and a judge will almost certainly find in his favor. You will be made to pay him approximately $1,050,000 to equalize the appreciation of the assets during the four years of marriage. The interim spousal support will end at that point in time."

"That's totally unacceptable."

"Life is hard, Beatrice. Perhaps next time you'll enter into a marriage contract before tying the knot or cohabiting. There's no point fighting. My recommendation would be to settle the matter quickly without going to court."

"You're a blunt little bastard, aren't you?"

"That's true but I really am trying to look after your best

interests. That's the end of the first part of our discussion. Now let's examine your contention that Johnathan is hiding assets. If we can prove it, the results will be much different."

CHAPTER 10 (Hidden Assets)

"Belinda's notes mentioned that you hired a private investigator to search for any assets that Johnathan might own which his lawyers hadn't disclosed. Did the fellow find anything?"

"He did not. He tailed Johnathan for several days and scoured the internet for relevant information but came up completely empty. I wasted several thousand dollars."

"Johnathan's attorneys provided a list of his assets as of the date of marriage. He owned no property or other investments, had no retirement plan and allegedly only had bank accounts worth about $20,000. Did you not realize at the time you met that he was close to being broke?"

"He had a very upscale lifestyle. Johnathan resided in an expensive condominium in Toronto, drove a Mercedes Benz and appeared to be exceedingly generous. We dined at the best restaurants during our courtship."

"Did you not discuss finances before deciding to get married?"

"We did but only in general terms. I raised the issue of a marriage contract but Johnathan felt that the very concept flushed a romance right down the drain. He convinced me that we were both wealthy enough to realize that our relationship was based on love and not the pursuit of a spouse's money."

"His tax returns indicate that Johnathan's income the year you met was only $35,000 and that he worked for a financial services company. He made no charitable donations and didn't show any other source of income."

"I was aware that he was in the investment business but Johnathan never disclosed that he was a low-level employee. He said that he lived off his dividends."

"Something is fishy. His stated income would be grossly insufficient to pay the rent on a pricey condo and lease a Mercedes Benz."

"That's my point exactly but Belinda Cartright was oblivious to my concerns. She kept droning on about needing proof of my allegations."

"Belinda was correct but tracing Johnathan's source of funds is the key to establishing that he's hiding his assets. Did he contribute to the living costs while you were married?"

"We kept our money completely separate but the answer to your query is yes. Although I continued to pay the house costs since the utilities and title were solely in my name, Johnathan paid for most of our entertainment expenses which were not insubstantial."

"You must have learned about Johnathan's lack of income once you were married because the tax returns of spouses must of necessity show the other spouse's income. Johnathan showed no personal income during those years. Was that not a red flag?"

"He explained that his corporation filed its own tax returns and that his accountants had advised Johnathan to keep his personal income at zero since the corporate tax rate was lower."

"Do you know the name of his company?"

"I'm sorry but I don't."

"It's unlikely that he even owns a corporation. He certainly doesn't mention anything like that on his financial disclosure forms."

"How can we find out for sure?"

"Did your private investigator contact Johnathan's former landlord in Toronto?"

"He did call them but they refused to divulge any information other than to confirm that Johnathan vacated with proper notice when he moved to Belleville."

"What did the investigator learn from Johnathan's former employer?"

"He discovered that Johnathan had only worked there for two years, was considered a decent

worker and left with two weeks'
notice around the time we got
engaged. The small firm had hired
Johnathan when they were desperate
for staff. As a result they didn't
have any résumé on file. Johnathan
had simply responded to their
newspaper advertisement. They
hired him on the spot. They did
have a notation in his file that
Johnathan claimed to have worked
for several years for a self-
employed accountant in Ottawa who
had recently died."

"How long were you engaged
before you got married?"

"It was only for a couple of
months after we had dated for
three months. We got married
quietly in Niagara Falls and
didn't invite anyone to the
ceremony."

"Do you know anything about
Johnathan's family?"

"He had none. His parents died
when Johnathan was in his early
twenties and he had been an only
child. He didn't even think he had
any aunts or uncles."

"Did you prepare new Wills after you got married?"

"I did because Richard advised me that my previous Will would be invalidated once I got married. Johnathan said that he'd use his own solicitor in Toronto to redo his Will."

"Did you make Johnathan your new beneficiary?"

"I did bequest a small portion of my estate to Johnathan but the bulk of it goes to my two daughters from my first marriage. To anticipate your next question, yes I've already changed my Will now that I'm separated."

"Did Belinda ask you similar questions?"

"No she did not. Her attitude was that she needn't get involved unless and until I provided her with proof of undisclosed assets."

"It's not a lot to go on, Beatrice. In the circumstances I would recommend two options. The first is to bite the bullet and pay Johnathan what his lawyers are demanding. That will save you substantial legal fees because you simply won't win if the matter goes before a judge."

"I hear you. What's the second option?"

"You and I can continue to examine Johnathan's affairs and attempt to discover how he was able to live a lavish lifestyle on such a paltry income. If we're successful in uncovering hidden assets, then you'll save money. If we hit a brick wall, then at some point relatively soon we'll have to give up our search and relegate the situation to the costly lesson learned file."

"That's the avenue I want to pursue."

"In that case, I'll need you to round up every morsel of information you've accumulated about Johnathan Jacobs. Don't omit anything. We need to see any credit card statements, receipts, correspondence or anything else that you still have in your possession."

We arranged that I'd return on Monday morning at nine o'clock.

I drove to the office and duly recorded the time I had spent with Beatrice today.

Richard was available so I dropped into his office and went over what Beatrice and I had discussed.

Next I got on the computer in my new office and searched Johnathan Jacobs on the internet. The results were surprisingly sparse. He had no social media presence.

I called it a day at four o'clock.

CHAPTER 11 (Leisure Time)

Quitting work at four o'clock seemed terribly decadent.

Restaurants were still locked down for indoor dining in Belleville so I was forced to cook my own supper. It would have been nice to go out for a sit-down meal.

In the evening I began checking out the estimated costs of opening my own law office.

To begin with I could operate the business without staff in which case the overhead would comprise mostly the rent, telephone and internet expenses.

Undoubtedly it would take months or even a couple of years to build up a clientele. Since family law was the main area of my expertise, it made sense to specialize in matrimonial work although Richard had indicated that real estate was a main staple of most sole practitioners.

The income I was earning on Beatrice's file was turning out to be an excellent stop-gap to sustain me while I navigated the obstacles to establishing my own office.

The delay while I worked for Richard would also provide me with the chance to learn about the city of Belleville.

On Saturday morning I drove all around the city getting my bearings.

Having the entire weekend free was a novel experience. At the old firm I had worked every Saturday and perhaps every other Sunday in order to maintain my billable hours.

My condominium complex was on the Belleville waterfront trail so in the afternoon I went on a long walk which took me downtown.

The pandemic seemed to be causing damage to a lot of businesses. There were many vacant stores in the downtown area.

Wearing a face mask wasn't required outdoors and I savored

the experience of walking without the facial covering which tended to fog up my glasses and irritate my skin in Toronto.

Beatrice was highly skeptical of the pandemic statistics and regulations and insisted that Richard and I not wear our face masks in her home.

Richard was also quite lenient and advised me that I only needed to wear a mask while seeing clients which I probably wouldn't be doing in any event since Beatrice was my only client at this time.

During my walk I felt the stirrings of anticipation that a fuller life might be just around the corner.

It was almost as if I had been released from a six year jail sentence.

Could romance be on the horizon?

On Sunday I actually slept in. After a late breakfast I went for another walk but this time I walked west on the Bay of Quinte ice.

Numerous other walkers had created a walking path although the packed-down snow was still a bit difficult to traverse. I accessed the waterfront trail walking path and used it to return to my condominium.

It was great to get a bit of exercise. I had been remiss in recent years. My crushing work hours had made it impractical to join a health club in Toronto.

In the evening I drank a couple of cans of beer and realized that Jimmy Corbett was knocking on the door of contentment.

Already I loved it here in Belleville.

CHAPTER 12 (Needles and Haystacks)

On Monday morning I arrived at Beatrice's home promptly at nine o'clock.

She had been busy over the weekend and had accumulated several boxes of material relating to Johnathan. Two of the boxes actually belonged to Johnathan but he had forgotten to take them when he moved out of the marital home.

"What should we be looking for?" Beatrice asked.

"You appear to know practically nothing about Johnathan's life before he began the job at the financial services company in 2014. Anything we discover about the prior years could help us solve the mystery of where he obtained the funds to live a lavish lifestyle despite earning about $35,000 in 2014 and 2015. That's one aspect we need to examine."

"I'm embarrassed that I could have been taken in by a scoundrel. I guess I was starved for love. My first husband had died five years earlier and Johnathan was my first foray back into the romance pool."

"Was the marriage to Johnathan enjoyable for a while?"

"It was. He was a very attentive gentleman at the beginning. I guess I'd have to admit that we had two good years before the relationship began to deteriorate. Have you ever been married?"

"I've never even been in love. After completing my education, work totally dominated my life. The past twelve days have been the most enjoyable period since finishing school. It's like I've been released from prison."

"I'm pleased for you, Jimmy. What else should we be looking for in these boxes?"

"It would be helpful to discover some evidence that Johnathan had other assets but I have no clue as to what form that evidence would take. I'd suggest that we each grab a box and begin examining the contents. Then we can switch boxes in order to have a second pair of eyes looking at everything."

That's how we proceeded.

I had no firm idea what to look for so simply hoped that I'd recognize something relevant once I saw it.

By mid-afternoon between us we had picked through all seven boxes. Beatrice had only managed to sort through the two boxes owned by Johnathan because she kept getting distracted by the material. Once or twice I noticed that she was close to tears.

The five boxes I examined didn't produce much useful information. One of them contained the written report of the private investigator which I carefully read.

"I'm exhausted," Beatrice moaned. "Let's pick up where we left off tomorrow morning. I didn't find anything useful and I'm feeling quite frustrated and exceedingly foolish. Did you locate any worthwhile information?"

"Your investigator spoke at length with Johnathan's employer in Toronto. That chap had written down in Johnathan's employee file the name of the deceased accountant Johnathan worked for in Ottawa. I'm going back to the office where I'll try to discover more about that accountant. Perhaps his family will be able to provide some details about Johnathan."

"At least we didn't completely waste our time today. That's a potential avenue of exploration."

CHAPTER 13 (Emergency)

Back at Richard's office, I got on the computer and attempted to track down the Ottawa accountant, a gentleman named Homer Townsend.

I found the fellow after a bit of digging and managed to locate his obituary.

With that information to work with, I discovered that his widow Ethel still lived at the same address.

Tomorrow morning I would attempt to contact Ethel.

Just as I was about to call it a day, Richard Kaufmann rushed into my office.

"Jimmy, we've got a crisis on our hands and I need you to step in and save us."

"That sounds ominous. What's up?"

"Belinda has a matrimonial trial commencing tomorrow morning but she suffered a panic attack about an hour ago and can't handle the stress. Her doctor just phoned. Belinda has to take a leave of absence for at least a month. The only other family law attorney in our firm was just called to the bar last June and simply doesn't have the experience to deal with this trial."

"I assume you want me to take over the trial."

"I do. The judge had already warned Belinda that she won't tolerate any more delays so postponing the trial isn't an option."

"Is Belinda well enough to explain the legal issues to me?"

"Her doctor won't allow it. I'm so sorry but you're our only hope."

"I'll need to call Beatrice. She expects me to show up tomorrow morning to continue our investigation into her ex-husband's affairs."

"I understand. Please be as diplomatic as possible with Beatrice. I'd call her myself but she seems to have taken a liking to you."

"I'll call her now while you bring me Belinda's file."

I phoned Beatrice and told her about my success in tracking down the accountant's widow.

"I had intended to phone the widow tomorrow but a crisis arose in the office. Belinda Cartright has taken sick and Richard needs me to take over a family law trial commencing in the morning. I'm so sorry but I may need to put your file on hold for a day or two. In the meantime perhaps you can examine the boxes of material that I sorted through to see if perhaps I missed some pertinent piece of the puzzle."

Beatrice was very accommodating and wished me luck in the trial.

Richard arrived with Belinda's file a few minutes later.

"Can Belinda's secretary provide me with any background?"

"I'm afraid not. Belinda's regular assistant moved out of the area just before Christmas and the replacement is very inexperienced. You're completely on your own."

"It is what it is. I'll study the file now and contact our client as soon as I can. Who is the opposing attorney?"

"It's a young sole practitioner named Astrid Brownell. I've never had a real estate deal with her and in fact I've only met her once about a year ago at a legal function shortly before the pandemic shut everybody down."

Richard departed and I picked up the file.

At least Belinda's notes and correspondence were detailed.

I began reading the letters from when the file was first opened in July of 2019.

The issues in dispute really weren't worth going to court over. It seemed that both attorneys got their backs up and refused to budge from their original positions.

In fact the animosity between the two lawyers was evident in the tone of the correspondence.

It only took me an hour to believe that I had a firm grasp on the file.

Since it was almost five o'clock, I decided to call Astrid Brownell before she left her office.

She answered her own telephone.

"Hello Astrid. My name is Jimmy Corbett and I'm employed temporarily at Richard Kaufmann's law firm. Belinda Cartright became sick this afternoon and will be on leave for at least a month."

"I'm not willing to postpone the trial. I'm sorry about Belinda but this file has been dragging on far too long."

"I understand. In fact Richard informed me that the judge won't allow any further extensions. I'm ready to handle the trial but before you left for the day, I thought it prudent to contact you and determine whether a last-minute settlement might be possible."

"What did you have in mind?"

"I've only had an hour to peruse the file but I'm a very experienced matrimonial litigation attorney. I worked for a mid-sized Toronto law firm for the past six years before deciding last month to leave the big city and get a life in a smaller town. I expect to establish my own law practice here in Belleville as soon as I've completed this temporary gig with Richard Kaufmann. The main issues in our dispute seem to be joint custody, the sale of the marital home and the amount of spousal support. I wanted to speak with you first before contacting our client."

"Mrs. Bertram is adamant that your client isn't capable of looking after the two young children because he's a workaholic. On the other hand, she works out of the family home. That's why she wants to purchase your client's interest in the house. I think Belinda tossed in the joint custody demand as a bargaining chip in reducing the amount of spousal support."

"From my initial reading of the correspondence, that tactic doesn't appear to have been successful."

"That's an understatement. It turned our respective clients into fixed statues refusing to budge on anything. Our only recourse was to let a judge sort it out."

"If I can persuade Mr. Bertram to accept reasonable access instead of joint custody, then he would have to pay the prescribed amount of child support instead of sharing those costs equally. Based on his income, I've calculated those costs to be $1,200 per month. How much of a reduction in the monthly spousal support would your client accept if Mr. Bertram was willing to pay that amount of child support?"

"I'm sure she would be flexible if your client allowed her to purchase the home from him."

"The value of the home seems to have been mutually agreed as

$540,000 and the outstanding mortgage is about $340,000. The equalization payment amount also doesn't appear to be in dispute. Mr. Bertram will pay his spouse $65,000. How would your client come up with the remaining $35,000 to buy out Mr. Bertram's share of the house?"

"Her parents are willing to loan her the money."

"Based solely on their respective incomes, after we deduct the monthly child support from Mr. Bertram, it doesn't appear that he would need to pay much spousal support to your client in order to fall within the established guidelines. Off the top of my head, I'd estimate it to be in the $1,000 per month range."

"That might fly if Mr. Bertram is amenable to accepting reasonable access instead of insisting on joint custody and if he is willing to sell his interest in the home to Mrs. Bertram."

"What was my client's reason for demanding that the home be sold? I couldn't figure that out from the file."

"It was pure spite. Mr. Bertram is a very difficult man."

"In that case I might have to offer him some incentive to be cooperative. Your client's business seems to be thriving despite the pandemic. Limiting the spousal support to three years might persuade my client to cave in on the house and custody issues."

"That doesn't seem too unreasonable. I know that custody is Mrs. Bertram's main concern with the house a close second."

"How do you want to proceed? Shall we call our respective clients now and run this tentative proposal by them?"

"It can't hurt but don't be surprised if Mr. Bertram tears a strip off you for alleged incompetence. Belinda loathed the man and couldn't get him to soften his position at all."

"Let's give it a try, Astrid."

CHAPTER 14 (Last Minute Settlement)

I phoned Carl Bertram and introduced myself.

As soon as I mentioned that Belinda Cartright had taken ill and was off on sick leave, Carl lost his temper and demeaned my abilities without knowing a single thing about me.

"Carl, you're damn lucky to have me. I've just moved to Belleville in order to set up my own legal practice. I bought a luxury condominium last week and used the services of Richard Kaufmann's office to handle my purchase. When Richard discovered that I had been an extremely experienced matrimonial litigation attorney in Toronto, he implored me to join his firm on a temporary basis so that I could handle a particularly complex divorce. Now earlier this afternoon he foisted your dispute onto my shoulders for the same reason. I just got off the phone with your wife's attorney and we've discussed a possible last-minute settlement."

"How can you possibly look after my interests adequately when you know nothing about my file?"

"That's the magic of experience, Carl. Your situation isn't particularly complicated. Here's my proposal. If you don't like it, then we'll take the matter to trial tomorrow and let the judge enforce her decision on your lives."

"I'm listening."

"I'll give you the summary first. Then we can discuss the specifics."

"Let me grab a pen and paper so I can jot down the details."

When Carl returned I began my spiel.

"Let's begin with the joint custody matter. I understand that you've got a very high-powered job."

"I work hard."

"I know the feeling. I put in eighty hour weeks for the past six years in Toronto and got sick of the career totally dominating my life. That's why I left the law firm earlier this month. The point I'm making is that with a demanding career, you're being unrealistic to want joint custody. Don't get me wrong. The judge will grant it to you because there's no reasonable evidence that you're unfit."

"That's another thing that drove me crazy. Alice had the gall to question my fitness as a father."

"Don't take it personally. It's a common legal tactic in a disputed divorce proceeding. The mild accusations contained in your file's correspondence don't mean a thing and mainly related to the long hours you work. My recommendation is to give in on the joint custody issue and accept reasonable visitation and access privileges. Since Alice works out of the home, she's in a far superior position to do the bulk of the child rearing duties."

"I'll think about it."

"While you're mulling over the custody issue, another area in which I suggest that we capitulate concerns the sale of the family home. What does it matter to you whether Alice buys you out and remains with the kids in the marital home?"

"It matters because the bitch is trying to buy me out with my own money."

"Alice is entitled to roughly $65,000 from you as the equalization payment. Apparently she can borrow the rest of the needed funds from her parents. Signing over your interest to Alice will save both of you real estate commission and even a bit of legal fees. At the $540,000 agreed value, the realty commission alone would be $30,510 inclusive of the Harmonized Sales Tax."

"What the hell is in it for me? You're caving in on everything."

"We're getting to that. If Alice gets sole custody of the kids, then you'll be obligated to pay her $1,200 monthly in total child support payments. That figure wasn't pulled out of the air. The government has a fixed schedule based on the non-custodial parent's income. The good news is that your monthly spousal support to Alice would be substantially reduced."

"I deeply resent paying anything to Alice. She earns good money."

"That's true but you earn quite a bit more because of the overtime you work. The judge won't take pity on you on that issue. I did discuss the possibility of limiting the spousal support to $1,000 monthly for a fixed term of three years."

"I like the sound of that. Facing the prospect of paying Alice forever really upset me. At some point I want to get on with my life. As it is I won't have enough money to purchase a decent house for myself."

"On the other hand, real estate prices are at historic highs right now and the economy looks to be on the brink of collapse. Renting might be a viable temporary option."

"What's your considered opinion of what you're proposing?"

"The financial aspects are excellent and likely better for you than what a judge would order, especially the time-limited spousal support. You're giving up joint custody which would almost certainly be awarded by the judge but from a guy's perspective, having your kids visit every other weekend is much less disruptive to your career than having them live with you every other week or month. There's another substantial cost saving for both you and Alice I haven't mentioned."

"What's that?"

"You won't be paying me $350 an hour for whatever number of days it takes to hash out these issues in court. Additionally, you and Alice can get on with your lives without the stress and hard feelings that a trial would generate."

"I suppose you want me to make a decision immediately."

"That's true. We've only got a few hours to reach an agreement and avoid the trial."

"I accept your terms. What happens next?"

"I'll call Alice's attorney back and let her know that we're agreeable to the proposal we discussed. By now she may have Alice's answer. I'll get back to you shortly. If it's a go, then the lawyers can exchange acceptance letters and I'll draft up the agreement tomorrow morning."

I managed to reach Astrid Brownell. Alice was also agreeable to the proposal.

"I have no life in Belleville yet, Astrid. I can bang off the Separation Agreement in the next hour and send it to you for approval."

"That would be wonderful. Perhaps we could even get the document executed this evening and be done with the matter."

I called Carl back and gave him the good news.

Then I pulled up the family law program and prepared a standard Separation Agreement reflecting the agreed-upon terms.

I e-mailed it to Astrid who checked it over and phoned me back with her approval.

To make a long story short, I had Carl come in to sign the agreement after which I drove the signed copies to Astrid's office where Alice was waiting to execute the document.

Twenty minutes later Astrid handed me our two signed copies of the agreement.

She phoned the court office and left a message on the judge's answering machine that we had settled the matter on the eve of trial.

"It's been a pleasure dealing with you, Astrid. Both of our

clients should be pleased with this compromise agreement."

"I fully agree. If the restaurants were open, I'd ask you to join me in a celebratory dinner."

"I'd love to take a rain check on that offer. Surely the province can't be shut down forever."

"It's a tentative date, then. Thanks for being so reasonable on this file, Jimmy. I really appreciated your sensible approach to the issues."

I left her office thinking that it had been a doubly successful accomplishment. In addition to getting the file settled, I also had my first tiny glimpse of possible romance.

Astrid was a lovely young lady with jet black hair and a slender figure.

Hope springs eternal even in the throes of a pandemic.

CHAPTER 15 (More Investigation)

On Tuesday morning I arrived at the office at eight o'clock in order to prepare the draft legal account for Carl Bertram's file.

Richard arrived just before nine o'clock and was thrilled that Belinda's file had been settled and the court trial avoided.

"Can I interest you in taking over all of Belinda's matrimonial files until she's back from her medical leave?"

"I can certainly help out because Beatrice's file won't keep me occupied for thirty-five hours a week. In fact we should know in a week or two whether there's any point in fighting her case. Beatrice is convinced that Johnathan has substantial hidden assets and we're trying to verify that matter but if we come up empty then it doesn't make economic sense for her to dispute the facts as they appear right now. Johnathan's demands are reasonable if in fact he has virtually no assets."

"I'll have Belinda's secretary round up her pressing files and discuss them with you."

Richard left and I phoned Beatrice to advise her that the emergency matrimonial matter had been settled last night which meant that I wasn't going to be in court all week. I advised her that I was going to phone the accountant's widow this morning.

Belinda's secretary popped in a few minutes later with three matrimonial files on which I might need to take some action. She tried to explain briefly the status of each file but as Richard had warned me yesterday, the girl was quite inexperienced.

I examined the files for an hour and then called Ethel Townsend, the widow of the accountant who employed Johnathan Jacobs for several years.

Ethel was very accommodating but her response was shocking.

Homer Townsend hadn't had any employees for the final seven years that he ran his accounting business and when he did have staff, they were all young women with the exception of Ethel who had been Homer's main secretary and assistant for most of his career.

Ethel had never met or heard of anyone named Johnathan Jacobs.

I thanked her for her help and rang Beatrice back with the interesting news.

"It's not solid evidence that we can use to locate Johnathan's assets but it does raise suspicions about him. Have you discovered anything relevant in the boxes I'd looked over?"

"No I haven't but I would like you to pore through the two boxes I looked at yesterday."

We arranged that I'd show up at one o'clock at Beatrice's home.

The thought crossed my mind that Beatrice was being charged $350 an hour for my time even though most of it had little or nothing to do with legal advice.

Primarily at the moment I was an extremely high-priced investigator rather than an attorney.

CHAPTER 16 (A Tiny Anomaly)

I arrived at Beatrice's house on time.

"Do you think Johnathan is some kind of con-man?" she asked.

"It's certainly suspicious that he lied to the Toronto financial firm about his work history. It also means that we know nothing about Johnathan's life before he began work for the financial firm. Are you sure that he never mentioned any specifics about his earlier life?"

"Johnathan was quite secretive about his past."

"While I'm looking through the two boxes belonging to Johnathan, perhaps you can jot down on a piece of paper anything you can recall that Johnathan said about his past. You must have inadvertently discussed events that happened when you were younger."

There were a lot of papers and miscellaneous records in the two boxes I began to sort through. It was no wonder that it had taken Beatrice so long to examine the contents last Friday.

In order to insert some semblance of order into the process, I began placing each item in separate piles.

The largest pile was irrelevant material into which I tossed anything that seemed unrelated to Johnathan's identity or finances.

Any receipts or bank statements went onto a separate pile and the third batch contained items related to his identity.

My first run through the boxes entailed only a cursory glance at each item while I assigned it to the applicable pile.

When I was finished after about ninety minutes, I packed the irrelevant pile back into one of the boxes.

My next target was the identity documents and I began to write out a profile for Johnathan Jacobs, who apparently had no middle name.

In an envelope labelled as photos, I began looking at the individual pictures which appeared to be of various flowers and trees. I had hoped to find some pictures of Johnathan and other people which might shed some light on Johnathan's past.

I was unfolding the last photo when a piece of paper fell out.

It was a photocopy of Johnathan's birth certificate indicating that Johnathan was born on April 7, 1962. His place of birth was shown as Springbrook, Ontario. I had no idea where that was so I googled it on my smart phone and discovered that it was a tiny village about twenty miles northwest of Belleville. His parents were shown as Minnie Wellman and Berend Jacobs.

That was useful information.

"Beatrice, did you know that Johnathan was born about twenty miles from Belleville in a tiny village called Springbrook?"

"No I didn't. He never mentioned where he had been born. How did you discover that?"

"A copy of his birth certificate was inside one of the folded photographs."

I took a closer look at the document.

"Here's something interesting. This birth certificate was issued in July of 2013 which was just a few months before he began working at the financial services business in Toronto."

"Why is that interesting?"

"It's odd that he would need a fresh copy of his birth certificate when he was fifty-one."

"What are you getting at, Jimmy?"

"Your comment about whether Johnathan was a con-man has stuck in my mind. Perhaps we can't unearth anything about Johnathan before his job in Toronto because he operated under a different name before then."

"That's a scary thought."

CHAPTER 17 (Startling Discovery)

I continued to pore through the pile of identity related materials.

Nothing seemed relevant to our search.

Next I tackled the pile of receipts and financial stuff.

The bulk of the material was credit card statements interspersed with a few receipts for items that Johnathan had purchased. Only a few of the items related to any period prior to his marriage to Beatrice.

One was a pay stub from the Toronto financial services firm which apparently was for Johnathan's first paycheck dated in October of 2013. Subsequent wages were deposited directly into his bank account.

A letter from his bank dated in the summer of 2013 welcomed Johnathan as a new customer and had apparently enclosed his new bank card.

When I had completed the evaluation of the various documents, I advised Beatrice that I was going to return to the office and take a closer look at any identification or financial materials which had been provided to Belinda by Johnathan's attorneys.

Back at the office I discovered that Johnathan's Ontario driver's licence had been issued in August of 2013. The opposing lawyer had provided us with a copy of it along with the income tax returns from 2014 to 2019 plus a rough estimated return for 2020.

Absolutely nothing in Belinda's file related to any period before the summer of 2013.

I phoned Beatrice and apprised her of my findings.

"I've had an idea which might prove to be useful. On a pleasant sunny day this week, I'd suggest that you drive up to Springbrook and see what information you can discover about Minnie and Berend Jacobs. As I mentioned to you at your home, Minnie's maiden name was Wellman."

"I'm no detective. How can I ferret out any information about them?"

"You might check the local cemetery for gravestones in their names. I checked the phone listings but found none in that general area for the surname Jacobs. Also, you might inquire at any of the local businesses. If there's a church in Springbrook perhaps you could obtain the names of some long-time village residents and contact them to discover if anyone recalls Minnie and Berend Jacobs or their son Johnathan."

"What is the purpose of that endeavor?"

"It's just an information gathering exercise. I have no idea whether you'll find out anything relevant or not."

Beatrice responded that she might drive to the village

tomorrow morning and bring along one of her daughters for company.

After we ended the call I pulled out one of Belinda's other matrimonial files and drafted a couple of letters to move that matter forward.

I left the office at five o'clock and cooked supper.

On Tuesday I was busy at the office with Belinda's other files.

With the time I was putting in, I hadn't had any opportunity to check out vacant offices or do anything else in preparation of opening my own legal practice.

Just past three o'clock the receptionist buzzed me that Beatrice Lantz was here to see me.

An excited Beatrice waltzed in and showed me on her smart phone some photos she had taken earlier today.

The results of her detective work had been startling.

She had taken pictures of the grave marker for Berend and Minnie Jacobs. The engravings confirmed that it was the correct people because Minnie was shown as Minnie Jacobs (nee Wellman).

Berend was shown as born in 1938 and died in 2008. Minnie showed born in 1939 and died in 2006.

The mind-blowing aspect was the much older engraving at the bottom of the marker which read "PARENTS OF BELOVED BABY JOHNATHAN JACOBS 1962-1964."

"Beatrice, this is crucial information. Johnathan must have stolen the identity of the infant child of Berend and Minnie. The man you married is definitely a fraud. That explains why nothing of Johnathan's predates 2013. That must be when he was successful in obtaining the birth certificate first and shortly thereafter his driver's licence and probably his social insurance number."

"What do we do now?"

"Let's get Richard Kaufmann in here if he's available. He's the boss and might want us to notify the police as well as the opposing attorney."

Richard was free to see us and he walked into my office a few minutes later.

CHAPTER 18 (Bizarre Complications)

We showed Richard what Beatrice had discovered earlier today.

Richard was flabbergasted.

"I've never encountered anything like this before. Family law is your specialty, Jimmy. Does this mean that Beatrice's marriage is invalid?"

"I'll have to do some research. There are so many bizarre possibilities. Johnathan might already have been married when he partook in the wedding ceremony with Beatrice in Niagara Falls. If he was, then the case law should be established regarding the validity of the Niagara Falls marriage."

"Does this mean that I won't owe the bastard one red cent?" Beatrice queried.

"That's another aspect that I'll need to research. Even if the wedding is declared invalid, you still cohabited with Johnathan for more than three years which presumably triggered a common-law spousal relationship. If that's the case, then the fact that the wedding ceremony might have been invalid won't alter the spousal financial obligations much if at all."

"That doesn't sound the least bit fair," Beatrice complained.

"A judge would hopefully take the fraudulent identity into consideration when determining whether any equalization payment was justified. The issue still remains unresolved regarding whether Johnathan owns assets in that name or in some previous identity."

"How do we determine that?" Richard asked.

"The best way would be to inform Johnathan's attorneys about this troubling new information and to set up an examination of discovery at which we can question Johnathan about his identity and regarding assets held under a different identity."

"Should we also be contacting the police?" Beatrice interjected.

"I believe we should. What do you think, Richard?"

"It does appear that a crime has been committed. I expect that we have a legal obligation to inform the police."

I suggested that we do a quick search of the criminal law aspects immediately.

The other two gathered around my computer as I attempted to learn a few basics.

It was clear that bigamy was a crime although at the moment we had no idea whether Johnathan was already married when he married Beatrice in 2016.

Identity fraud was also a crime.

It seemed that Johnathan had committed several crimes in that regard. Obtaining the birth certificate and subsequently using it to obtain his Ontario driver's licence was definitely a crime. Presumably Johnathan had also used that birth certificate to obtain a social insurance number in the name of Johnathan Jacobs.

Getting married to Beatrice using phony identification was also a type of fraud under the Criminal Code.

We discussed which police department to contact and decided that the Ontario Provincial Police was as good a place as any to start.

I phoned the local detachment and explained the situation to the receptionist who put the call through to a detective.

That woman agreed to meet us at Beatrice's home in thirty minutes.

Richard had appointments for the remainder of the afternoon so Beatrice and I drove in separate vehicles to her house.

The police detective arrived on time and we provided her with the information we had uncovered so far which included a copy of Johnathan's Ontario driver's licence and birth certificate along with his social insurance number, his current address as well as that of his attorney. I also gave the detective a copy of the marriage certificate which was in Belinda's divorce file.

"You're the first person we've contacted about these crimes but when I return to my law office, I'm going to send an email to Johnathan Jacobs' attorney in Toronto apprising him of the complex issues which have just been revealed and disclosing that we've referred the criminal matters to the Ontario Provincial Police. Can I provide the lawyers with your contact information?"

The detective had no problem with me advising the opposing divorce lawyers of these developments and telling them that Detective Anita McCready was the investigating officer at this point in time.

I drove back to the office and banged off a letter to Johnathan's lawyers briefly setting out our recent discoveries and admitting that they greatly complicated the divorce file. I touched on the issue of possible bigamy and pointed out that the fact that Johnathan Jacobs was a phony identity vastly increased the chances that Johnathan had assets hidden away under another name given the fact that he was living an upscale life at the time he met Beatrice.

I emailed the letter to the opposing attorney whose name was Grant Peden and also explained that I had taken over the file from Belinda Cartright who was off on sick leave.

Since it was by then after five o'clock, I went home.

CHAPTER 19 (Disappearing Act)

On Thursday morning when I arrived at the office, there was a telephone message from Grant Peden in Toronto.

I returned the call and Peden picked up immediately.

For a matrimonial litigation attorney, he was quite amicable.

"Thanks a lot for turning a standard matrimonial file into a nightmare," Peden quipped.

"It stunned me as well. I've never encountered anything like this before. Have you spoken with the mysterious Johnathan Jacobs since receiving the bad news?"

"I reached him by telephone last evening around seven o'clock but the conversation was entirely unpleasant. Jacobs or whatever his real name is got spooked when I disclosed that you had contacted the Ontario Provincial Police who were now investigating the matter.

He fired me on the spot and called me every name in the book."

"That's probably a good thing in the circumstances."

"I totally agree. Fortunately we had his retainer in our trust account so most of our legal account will be paid. The purpose of this call is to advise you that we no longer represent Johnathan Jacobs and that presumably he will contact you through another attorney if he decides to pursue his spousal claim against Beatrice Lantz."

"I'm surprised you didn't persuade him to stick with your firm. Your criminal section could have earned big bucks out of the complex maze of laws Johnathan broke."

"We don't handle criminal matters in the firm. It's too specialized an area and doesn't mesh well with the other types of files we do take on. Your client should be pleased with this new development. It greatly reduces the chances that she'll be made to cough up any equalization payment to Mr. Jacobs."

"That's true but it will certainly complicate the divorce unless we can establish that Johnathan was still married to someone else when he tied the knot with Beatrice. Something tells me Johnathan Jacobs has already gone underground. I'd bet you anything that the police will discover that he's flown the coop."

"That wouldn't surprise me. In any event, good luck with the matter. I'll send you an email confirming that we spoke and that I duly informed you that this firm is no longer representing the individual calling himself Johnathan Jacobs."

As soon as Grant Peden and I ended our phone call, I rang Detective McCready and brought her up to speed.

She thanked me for the information and shared the same opinion as me that Johnathan Jacobs would not be apprehended.

Finally I called Beatrice Lantz and told her about my phone calls with Grant Peden and with Detective McCready.

"What do you suggest that I do now, Jimmy?"

"For the time being it would make sense for you to do nothing. I doubt that Johnathan is going to pursue his claim for equalization relief. That's the good news. Rather than seek a divorce for cause at this time, I'd recommend that you wait until you've been legally separated for a year and then have us apply for a divorce."

"What if we or the police learn that Johnathan was already married when he purported to marry me?"

"In that case you can contact us and we'll apply for an annulment. There's no point in having us run up your legal account. I'll prepare an interim account covering everything the firm has done for you up to now and Richard will return the balance of the retainer to you."

"I can't thank you enough for your work, Jimmy."

"Quite frankly it was your own detective work that solved the problem."

"It was at the very least a team effort. You were the one who found the birth certificate and got the ball rolling on the fake identity possibility."

For the rest of the week I worked on other matrimonial files.

The following Monday I got a call from Beatrice Lantz.

Detective McCready had just contacted Beatrice to inform her that Johnathan Jacobs had disappeared by the time the police arrived at his apartment on Saturday morning with a warrant for his arrest.

The detective was of the opinion that Johnathan was a veteran con-man and would never be apprehended. She expected that he had already changed his appearance and was utilizing another set of false identification documents.

McCready had lamented that professional fraudsters seemed always to be two steps ahead of law enforcement.

Beatrice thanked me again for my assistance on her file.

CHAPTER 20 (Life Goes On)

Richard Kaufmann took me out to lunch on Monday, the 1st of February. He indicated how pleased he was with the quality of my legal work and tried to persuade me to join his law firm.

The pay package he was willing to give me was generous, comprising a base salary of $125,000 plus twenty percent of my gross billings and he emphasized that he wouldn't expect me to work more than fifty hours in most weeks.

I told Richard that I appreciated his offer and would definitely think about it but that I still had a strong desire to be my own boss and have complete control over my work life.

Belinda's matrimonial files kept me occupied over the next ten days.

On February 10th this section of Ontario was moved into the Covid-

19 Green Zone which meant that restaurants could reopen for indoor dining although only at twenty-five percent capacity.

The following day I received a rare evening phone call at my condo.

"Hello Jimmy. This is Astrid Brownell. Do you remember me?"

"Of course I do Astrid. It's nice to hear from you. What's new in your life?"

"Business has been relatively quiet but that has given me a chance to catch up with my book-keeping records. Are you still working at Richard Kaufmann's office?"

"I am. The primary file I was hired to look after seems to have been resolved but Belinda Cartright is off on medical leave at the moment so I've been handling her files until she returns."

"When do you think that will happen?"

"I expect that she'll return in a week or so."

"What will you do then?"

"I haven't completely decided. Richard has offered me a job but I still seem to have an urge to set up my own practice. The restaurants are open again and I'd love to pick your brain about what it's like to operate your own law firm. Can I entice you to join me for dinner tomorrow evening?"

"That would be great. In fact that's why I phoned you. We tentatively made plans to get together once the lockdown was over."

We chatted for a bit longer, mostly about the lockdowns and what effect we expected them to have on the Canadian economy in general and our own profession in particular.

We both felt that it was too early to really know.

Friday was relatively busy at the office and I was pleased when the workday ended.

Astrid and I had made arrangements to meet at five-thirty at The Boathouse, a seafood restaurant on the Belleville harbor near the downtown section of the city.

I parked on the street near the restaurant and was escorted to a small table.

Astrid arrived a few minutes later, spotted me and came over to the table where she removed her face mask.

We made small talk for a few minutes about our respective days at the office.

When the server arrived, Astrid mentioned that she didn't drink alcohol. We both ordered soft drinks to go with our food selection.

"You said that you've had your own legal practice here in town for two years. Have you always operated at your current location?"

"Yes. I signed a five-year lease."

"Do you not have a secretary?"

"My business hasn't grown enough yet to justify staff. It's not easy attracting clients even though I grew up in the nearby town of Trenton."

"How much rent are you paying?"

"It sets me back $1,800 a month plus hydro. The rest of my overhead runs about $1,000 each month but that includes my Ontario Law Society dues and my errors and omissions insurance."

"Don't answer if I'm being too intrusive, but how much are you able to bill out on an average month?"

"In 2020 my total billings were just over $54,000 and my total overhead was about $31,000. I'm not getting rich but in 2019 I earned less than $6,000 because I had only opened my office in June of that year."

"Do you work long hours?"

"Since I'm the only one in the office, I really have to be there all day. I tend to do banking and other errands during the lunch period. Generally I bring my own sandwich for lunch. It's a bit of a struggle but I enjoy the relative control I have over my life. Just between you and me, I wish I hadn't committed myself to a five year office lease. The space is too large but I foolishly expected to thrive right out of the gate. Are you sure you want to run your own office?"

"You're an excellent attorney, Astrid. It is a bit disappointing to realize that it takes significant time to build up a law practice. Do you handle legal matters other than family law?"

"Although I haven't had one walk in the door yet, I will take on automobile accidents and slip and fall cases. I also just decided last month to expand my areas of practice to include real estate transactions."

"That's interesting. What made you arrive at that decision?"

"I spoke with two other young attorneys who operate their own law offices and they convinced me that handling real estate deals really helps cash flow and also that real estate is generally a happy branch of the law. Folks are excited because they're buying a home or selling one and getting a boatload of cash in their hands. But the main reason for taking on a wider spectrum of business is because I need to generate more billings."

"That's good to know. Sticking with Richard Kaufmann would certainly make monetary sense in the near term but I'm concerned that in order to earn my wages I'd gradually have to increase my work hours. In Toronto I was extremely well paid but I had to work obscene hours. Most weeks I logged in at least eighty hours and that made having a normal life impossible."

"How well paid were you?"

"My annual salary was $302,000 plus a smallish Christmas bonus. Richard already warned me that I'd never make that kind of money in Belleville whether I worked for a law firm or operated my own office."

"Does that upset you?"

"I'm reasonably comfortable financially, mainly because I sold my house in Toronto for a great price early last month and also because I had no opportunity to spend the great salary I was earning. Six solid years on that treadmill was plenty."

"Do you rent an apartment in Belleville?"

"No, I purchased a condominium unit at Pier 31 as soon as I arrived here. The prices seemed miraculously low in Belleville and now I feel like a gentleman of wealth."

"That's impressive. I'm still renting and prices have risen so drastically since I opened my own office that I'm beginning to worry that I'll never be able to afford my own house."

"The house in Toronto was my only major purchase while I was there. I didn't even own a vehicle for the last few years until last month when I purchased an older model car. My home was within walking distance of the law firm's offices and was also on a bus route."

We continued chatting while we ate our supper.

The server seemed to be encouraging us to leave to open up the table for other diners. Restaurants could only operate at twenty-five percent capacity.

"I guess we should leave, Astrid. Would you like to see my condominium? I can brew a pot of coffee and we can continue our conversation."

"That would be lovely, Jimmy."

That's what we did.

I was very comfortable with Astrid. When we noticed that it was almost midnight, we ended the evening but arranged to go out for dinner again next Friday.

We didn't kiss goodnight but I got the distinct impression that Astrid liked my company. I had certainly enjoyed myself tonight and was greatly looking forward to seeing Astrid again.

CHAPTER 21 (Decision Time)

Monday was the Family Day holiday in Ontario so I had the day off.

On Tuesday afternoon Richard Kaufmann wandered into my office and sat down across from me.

"Belinda spoke with me this morning, Jimmy. She's feeling better now and is ready to return to work immediately. I told her that she can start tomorrow morning. That brings us to your situation. Belinda will need her office back but you're welcome to remain with the firm and can use the office you started with when your only file was Beatrice Lantz's matrimonial dispute. Have you made a decision about your future?"

"I gave the matter a lot of thought over the long weekend. As generous as your offer is, I have a strong desire to open my own law office. I do want to thank you for letting me work here for the past month. It has allowed me to meet some of the other attorneys in town and learn a bit more about Belleville. When would you like me to leave your employ?"

"It would be helpful if you could stay until the end of the week in order to bring Belinda up to speed on what's happened with her current files."

"I'm happy to stay until Friday, Richard. That will give me plenty of time to show Belinda whatever progress has been made on her files."

"When do you expect to open up your own law office?"

"I'll need to find office space first but I'd be surprised if I'm not up and running by the 1st of March."

"I wish you all the success, Jimmy. You've proven yourself to be a tremendous attorney just in the short time you've worked here. I really am sorry to see you leave the firm."

Richard made sure that he squeezed every ounce of work out of me over the course of the remainder of the week.

In fact he asked me to come back after supper each day except Friday.

The good news was that he paid me a bonus of $2,000 in addition to my regular pay.

By Friday at five o'clock when I said goodbye to those of the staff I had met, I was quite exhausted. The extra two hours spent at the office each evening had brought back memories of the Toronto law firm.

It did however reinforce my decision to open my own office. I had been correct. Working for Richard would quickly have turned into the same daily grind I had endured in Toronto.

For my date with Astrid, I picked her up in my car and we drove to the Royal Haveli Indian Restaurant on Bell Blvd. in the north end of the city.

"I'm suddenly unemployed," I announced once we had sat down.

"What happened?"

"Belinda came back to work on Wednesday so Richard didn't require my services after today. He also made me work in the evenings but he compensated me by paying a nice bonus. I'm glad I had the temporary work opportunity but I'm even more convinced that setting up my own office is the wisest choice."

"Have you given any thought to where you'll rent your office?"

"I've been a bit too busy to investigate available rentals. I hope I'll be able to find a spot similar to yours. You're situated in a small strip plaza with ample parking space and where free parking is also allowed on the street."

Astrid's office was on South Front Street right across the street from The Moorings which was one of the condominiums I looked at when I first arrived in town.

There were only two other small businesses in the plaza. One of them was a charitable foundation office and the third space was occupied by a driver's education company.

In fact the location was even within reasonable walking distance to the court house.

"I've just had an interesting thought," Astrid commented.

"What's that?"

"I've got way more space than I need. There's plenty of room for a second attorney and some secretarial staff. Would you be at all interested in that sort of arrangement?"

"That might work out well for both of us. Do you have the right to sublet a portion of your space?"

"Yes I do. I made sure of that when I signed the lease because I insisted on the option to share the office with another attorney."

"One possible complication comes to mind which I suppose we should discuss before we made any other decisions."

"What complication is that?"

"I'm not sure how to phrase it properly without seeming creepy or presumptuous. I enjoy your company but I'm very rusty when it comes to social situations. I've assumed that tonight is an actual date. If we did happen to connect romantically, then sharing office space would make perfect sense. If on the other hand our possible relationship fizzled, then it might be highly uncomfortable occupying the same office."

"Are you saying that it's a bad idea to share office space?"

"I guess I'm saying that I'd rather find my own office space if sharing space meant that we couldn't continue to see each other socially. I came to Belleville to live a fuller life than I had in Toronto and finding romance is a big part of that dream."

"I think I'm flattered. You do make a good point, however. I'm sure we've both learned first-hand from our jobs how nasty things can get when a couple splits up. So far I really enjoy being with you but it's definitely early days as far as whether this will blossom into a romance. Let's think about it for a few days."

"It can't hurt for us to meet at your office tomorrow and evaluate the specifics. It's possible that the layout of your office space won't be conducive to accommodating two lawyers in which case we're putting the cart before the horse. Even though I was there briefly when we were dealing with that matrimonial file, I didn't pay much attention to your office."

For the rest of the evening we talked about our childhoods and university days.

This time we did kiss goodnight when I drove Astrid home. I thoroughly enjoyed the experience but wondered how wise it was to enhance the romance while we were considering a business arrangement.

It took me a long time to get to sleep.

This was decision time but my thoughts were quite muddled.

CHAPTER 22 (Office Mates)

On Saturday morning I made breakfast and then drove to Astrid's office. She hadn't arrived yet.

A few minutes later Astrid drove in to the plaza.

As she got out of the car she moaned.

"It's been a terrible morning. The old home where I rent my apartment had no heat or hot water when I woke up. The place was frigid. Apparently a repairman is coming soon but I wasn't able to shower. I must look a mess."

"You look gorgeous, Astrid."

"You're such a liar," she retorted with a chuckle.

We evaluated the available space. It was very suitable for two separate legal offices.

The front door was at the south end of the office space. A client entering was greeted by a reception area. A secretary would sit behind a desk facing the entrance and there were four chairs to the north of the front door for clients to sit on while waiting to be seen by the lawyer.

A wall with a doorway in the middle was set about fifteen feet behind the front door.

Astrid left that door open so that she could hear anyone entering even when she was in her own office working.

Once passing through the doorway, there were four offices, two on each side of the hallway.

At the end of the hallway there was an open storage room on one side and the washroom on the other side with a rear exit door in the center which led to the back of the small plaza.

I opened the back door to discover that there were an additional twelve parking spaces which was a nice surprise.

Astrid informed me that the plaza owner looked after snow removal.

"The layout is excellent to accommodate two legal offices," I admitted.

"I know. Have you had any epiphanies about the wisdom of combining a possible romance with an office sharing arrangement?"

"I did give it a lot of thought. Now that I've seen how well suited the office space is, I'm inclined to risk the possibility that the romance will fizzle in which case we would hopefully remain friends and business associates."

Astrid burst out laughing but I had no idea why.

I looked at her curiously.

Finally she explained.

"You are definitely naïve when it comes to romance, Jimmy. If we fell in love and then one of us wanted to end the relationship, the acrimony would be dreadful. Being stuck in the same office space would be a nightmare."

"I guess that's a valid point. I've only had a handful of dates since I left law school. The hours I worked left no time for a social life. In fact I haven't had a steady girlfriend since I was in university. What about you?"

"I certainly had my share of boyfriends in university and law school but quite frankly you're the first guy I've liked since I moved to Belleville and opened the office."

"I've always been a rebel. As far as I'm concerned, the law of restricted choice was meant to be broken."

"I don't follow you, Jimmy."

"That law would dictate that we have only two choices, pursue the romance and get separate office space or end the romance and share this office. In fact I'm mildly optimistic that we can successfully have both a romance and a shared office arrangement. If the relationship tanks, then we need to be adults about it and not let ourselves get bitter."

"I was hoping you'd say that and I agree. The office sharing will be hugely beneficial to both of us and we should definitely do it. As far as our potential romance, it's too early to predict what will happen but so far I like our chances of really connecting."

"It's settled then. I'll start paying my half of the rent immediately. Where's a good place to buy used office furniture?"

"We can start at Barratt's which is downtown. But first I need to give you a welcome to my office kiss to seal our deal."

That kiss lasted a deliciously long time and by the time it ended I was convinced that I was making the right decision.

Two of the offices were completely empty. Astrid's own personal office was furnished but the final office only contained one four-drawer filing cabinet.

The photocopier, fax machine and scanner were all in the receptionist's space. Astrid had two desktop computers, one on the desk in the front room and the other in her own office.

"Does it make much sense for you to obtain your own telephone and fax numbers in addition to duplicating the office equipment?" Astrid queried.

"What are you suggesting?"

"To keep costs down, it might be wiser to share the phone and fax as well as the other office equipment."

"That would tend to mean a partnership. Is that really a good move for you? You've already got a clientele whereas I'm starting completely from scratch."

"We could arrange it so that we share the office costs equally but keep our individual billings separate?"

"I see what you're getting at. Would we turn it into a limited liability partnership or keep it as a standard partnership?"

"We could try it out for a few months as a standard partnership and change it after we determine whether the cost of a limited liability partnership makes economic sense."

"I like that idea, Astrid. It also means that I can be up and running as a practising attorney as early as Monday morning."

"Then that's what we'll do, partner. Now let's make a list of the equipment and furniture you'll need to get started."

CHAPTER 23 (Room-Mates)

I was quite excited as Astrid and I went from room to room determining what furniture and equipment I'd need.

We decided that I would purchase a half share in the existing computers and office equipment and that we would split the cost of anything else we needed.

For the time being I would occupy the receptionist's desk and use that computer.

In the end we postponed any additional purchases until we had a chance to better evaluate our needs.

Since Astrid had skipped breakfast, we got take-out food and drove to my place so that Astrid could shower after we'd eaten our lunch.

Next I drove with Astrid to her apartment so that she could discover whether the heat and water problems had been repaired yet.

The news was disheartening.

I listened as her landlord, who also resided in the home, gave Astrid the bad news.

"We've got a terrible problem, Astrid. The pipes have now burst because of the lack of heat. Gail and I have to move out immediately and so will you. The city has shut off the water to stop the water damage but there's still water in some of the pipes. It's going to take weeks if not months to make the repairs and the building is uninhabitable until then. I've sent my son to pick up a moving truck which should arrive shortly. We've got to move your furniture out of the apartment before everything is ruined."

"I can't find another apartment today," Astrid moaned.

"Do you have room in your office for the furniture?" the owner inquired.

"I suppose I do."

Just then the small moving truck pulled up. The landlord excused himself to direct his son where to park.

"This is just awful," Astrid complained. "I can't live in our office."

"As the old English saying goes, in for a penny, in for a pound," I responded. "If we're going to be law partners, we may as well live together as well. You can take either the north bedroom or use the third floor loft area as your sleeping quarters."

"Are you sure, Jimmy? We've had like two dates. Are we nuts to go from a casual relationship into one in which we're glued to each other twenty-four hours a day?"

"Circumstances seem to be pushing us in that direction. The condo is plenty large enough to enable each of us to have our own space."

"It's by far the easiest option. If we quickly get sick of each other, then at least we will have proven that we're not compatible.

Seriously though, if being in such close quarters turns out to be a problem, then please tell me right away."

"You worry too much, Astrid. Let's get your stuff moved onto the truck before the water does any further damage."

It only took an hour to remove all of Astrid's furniture and belongings. A few items were wet but seemingly undamaged. Unfortunately Astrid's box spring and bed were ruined but that was the extent of the bad news. She stuffed her clothes and some other items into my car while the landlord's son and I carried the furniture from the rear apartment to the moving truck.

Then the son in the truck followed Astrid and me to Pier 31 where we unloaded everything in less than an hour.

We thanked him and he went back to his parents' home to move their own furniture out of the house.

Astrid and the landlord had already come to an agreement that the tenancy was terminated and that he would mail the balance of the February rent to Astrid at her law office. She hadn't paid any rental deposit when she first moved in and the utilities were included in her monthly rent.

Astrid had no apartment insurance but she admitted that she had purchased the bed and mattress used and that they were close to worthless.

We had a pizza delivered for supper.

I was quite excited about the prospect of living with Astrid.

Moving to Belleville had quickly provided me with the better life I had craved while chained to my desk in Toronto.

CHAPTER 24 (A Taste of Bliss)

The sleeping arrangements were dictated by the fact that Astrid's bed had been destroyed.

The sellers had left me their own spare bed up in the third floor loft because it had been so difficult to squeeze the box spring up the bend in the staircase leading to the loft.

That meant that the law of restricted choice again ruled the day.

We spent the evening moving Astrid's furniture from location to location until she was satisfied with the layout.

It was fortunate that the condo had been so sparsely furnished when I bought it and that I hadn't had the time or inclination to go out and buy items to fill in the empty spaces.

In fact the loft area was huge and Astrid seemed thrilled with it. The sellers had left a bookshelf and desk on the top floor in addition to the bed and two soft armchairs.

The only thing missing up there was a closet so Astrid hung some of her clothes in the walk-in closet off my second floor master bedroom and the rest in the front room closet.

We did manage to carry her chest of drawers and bedside night tables up to the loft by first removing the drawers. That meant that any clothing items which couldn't be hung up in a closet could fit in the drawers where Astrid would have easy access.

I hadn't bothered to purchase a television but now we could use Astrid's flat-screen TV as soon as we hooked it up to a cable service.

When we were tired from sorting out the furniture, we brewed some coffee and sat in the living-room.

"I think the move went remarkably smoothly," I commented.

"You're right about that. Who could have predicted that last night we led completely separate lives and now just a day later we're business partners and shacking up together? I hope you're not getting spooked already."

"I'm thrilled with these developments, Astrid. From my own point of view it seems that the more rounded life which had seemed completely out of reach in Toronto is rapidly being realized in Belleville."

"I'm pretty excited about everything as well despite the fact that we've compressed so many relationship phases into a single day."

On Sunday we concentrated on our partnership agreement and wrote up a very simple document which we signed in order to fulfil any legal or taxation requirements which dictated that a law office partnership had to be in written form.

During the ensuing week we ordered business cards and new office signs. We called the partnership BROWNELL & CORBETT because Astrid was already shown in the phone book.

Each evening our goodnight kiss grew longer and more passionate.

Finally on Friday night Astrid slept with me in the master bedroom.

The closeness we felt was magical and we knew that in fact we hadn't rushed things after all.

We were absolute soul-mates.

CHAPTER 25 (Unwanted Intruder)

Beatrice Lantz received a phone call from Detective McCready on Tuesday, the 23rd of February.

"There's been a breakthrough in tracking down the true identity of Johnathan Jacobs. Our forensic team dusted his apartment for fingerprints after they determined from the landlord that the unit seemed to be abandoned."

"What did you find out?"

"He's in the system. His real name is Arnold Kowalski and he is originally from Akron, Ohio. His only conviction was in 2003 for various financial scams in the USA and he served three years in a minimum security facility in New York State. As soon as he was released, Mr. Kowalski vanished and hadn't resurfaced until you discovered that his current identity as Johnathan Jacobs was fraudulent."

"Why did you use the term 'his only conviction'?"

"Kowalski was charged on two earlier occasions with aggravated assault causing bodily harm and once with manslaughter but he wasn't convicted. It appears that he was much more dangerous long before he took the alias Johnathan Jacobs."

"That's rather horrifying and doesn't say much for my ability to judge character. I'm humiliated to have actually married the creep."

"Don't beat yourself up about it, Ms. Lantz. Con artists are diabolically adept at portraying sophistication and virtuous characteristics. It's what they do best."

"Thank you for updating me with this new information, Detective McCready. I really do appreciate it."

When Beatrice got off the phone, she thought it prudent to advise Jimmy Corbett about this latest development.

She phoned Richard Kaufmann's office only to discover that Jimmy no longer was employed there.

Beatrice had Jimmy's smart phone number so she contacted him that way.

They spoke for several minutes and Jimmy divulged that he had entered into a law partnership with an attorney named Astrid Brownell and that their office was on South Front Street.

Beatrice wished Jimmy all the best in his new venture and promised to direct business his way if the opportunity arose.

On Saturday Beatrice had lunch with her daughter at a restaurant in Trenton and returned home shortly after one o'clock.

She hung up her winter coat and went upstairs to brush her teeth.

As Beatrice entered the bedroom, she came face to face with Johnathan who was trying to pry open the wall safe which was hidden behind a painting.

"How did you get in?" Beatrice asked frantically.

"I knew you'd be too cheap to change the locks. My key still worked so I didn't have to break in."

"What do you want?"

"What does it look like I want? I'm here to confiscate the gold and silver coins you keep stashed in the safe. Now that you're here, you can save me a ton of effort. Open the damn safe."

"No."

Beatrice opened her purse and pulled out her smart phone with the intention of calling 911 but Johnathan snatched it away from her and knocked her onto the floor with a vicious punch.

"Don't make me kill you, Beatrice. I just want the coins plus whatever cash you've got lying around. Then I'll be out of your life permanently."

Beatrice tried to recall what she had learned years ago at a seminar about how to react when being accosted by a thief. The instructor had emphasized that the best approach was to comply with the robber's request.

"I'll open the safe. Except for the money in my purse, the only other cash in the house is inside the safe."

Beatrice's hands were shaking as she worked the combination. In fact she got it wrong the first time much to the annoyance of Johnathan who warned her that he would kill her if she continued to waste his time and patience.

Even Johnathan's voice was different. It was hard and rather common, just the opposite of the sophisticated intonation he had used while they were married.

Johnathan pushed her aside when Beatrice swung the small door of the wall safe open.

He had a sports bag into which he stuffed the loot. When he had extracted everything he felt he could use, Johnathan dug into Beatrice's purse and helped himself to the cash in her wallet.

"I'm going to have to tie you securely in order to give myself enough time to get well out of this area. Don't give me any lip or I'll silence you permanently. The useless cops in this two-bit hick town would never suspect me. They'll put the robbery down to the work of a local drug addict."

Beatrice opted to be compliant.

She was a bit concerned when Johnathan pulled out some plastic restraints from his bag along with some type of strong-looking rope. He had come prepared.

Beatrice allowed Johnathan to secure her wrists and ankles which he did while she was lying prone on the bed.

Then he tied her to the bedposts in a manner from which she had no chance of escaping.

Just when Beatrice prayed that Johnathan would just take his booty and leave, the situation worsened.

Johnathan extracted a handgun equipped with a silencer.

"I'm a betting man, Beatrice. You didn't know that about me, did you? I like to take risks. In fact

I live for the thrill of putting it all on the line. My original plan was to kill you while we were married but the perfect opportunity never arose. That's when I devised the idea of tolerating your pompous company for at least three years and milking you legally through the separation agreement. It seemed to be working perfectly until my attorney called to inform me that I was a fraud and no longer worthy of his legal representation. Don't take it personally but I'm going to kill you now."

"Why would you do that Johnathan? You've got my gold and my cash. As you said yourself, by the time I'm found, you'll be long gone."

"That's true but it just struck me that letting you live would mean that I'm forever on the run from being apprehended and charged with a serious crime. Killing you increases the odds exponentially that the police would never suspect me. That's why I'm wearing latex gloves. Despite your wealth and lofty position in this town, I've always been smarter than you."

Beatrice was frantic.

Johnathan raised the gun to shoot her.

Beatrice had to do something.

"Don't flatter yourself, Johnathan. You might have outsmarted me but my attorney was incredibly more intelligent than you. He's the one who discovered that your identity was fake."

CHAPTER 26 (The Spider and the Fly)

The distraction worked at least temporarily.

"Don't try to con me, Beatrice. That bitch you hired was useless. Even my own lawyer joked about how desperately the timid Ms. Cartright wanted to settle my claim. It was your cheapness that compelled you to drag out the negotiations. Brilliant legal representation had nothing to do with it."

"I dumped Belinda Cartright and hired a young man named Jimmy Corbett. Whereas Belinda accomplished nothing in the four months she acted on my behalf, Jimmy was a magician and quickly proved how an astute attorney can work wonders. Within a week Jimmy had pierced your flimsy veil of deceit and cracked the case. You were simply no match for him."

"I don't believe you."

"If Belinda was still representing me, by now I would have caved in and paid you what your attorneys were demanding. Jimmy saved me at least a million bucks. It looks good on you. Johnathan Jacobs was bested by a young lawyer. I can die satisfied now knowing that your evil plan to confiscate some of my wealth crashed and burned because you were so quickly humiliated by my attorney."

Beatrice watched Johnathan as he paced back and forth in the massive bedroom while he decided what to do.

Finally he opened his sports bag and extracted some wide tape.

"Close your disgusting cheapskate mouth," he demanded as he taped her mouth shut.

Then she observed him examining her smart phone.

A diabolical smile suddenly filled his face.

"Congratulations, you miserable bitch. You've just signed Mr. Corbett's death warrant. I'm going to make you watch me while I shoot the loser right here in this room. Then when I'm satisfied that you fully realize what your big mouth has caused, I'll put a bullet right in your brain pan."

Johnathan punched in some numbers while a horrified Beatrice watched helplessly.

...

My smart phone buzzed on Saturday afternoon just before two o'clock.

"Good afternoon. This is Jimmy Corbett."

"Hello, Mr. Corbett. My name is Michael Ackermann and I'm employed by the accounting firm which looks after Beatrice Lantz's financial affairs. I'm at her home now poring over some records and some queries have arisen about the legal work you did recently for Beatrice."

"I'm no longer employed by the Kaufmann law firm and they're in possession of Beatrice's legal file. You probably should speak with Belinda Cartright. It's unlikely that I can shed much light on whatever questions you have about the matter."

"Actually I just contacted Ms. Cartright but she was unable to provide me with the answers and recommended that I call you. It's too complicated to explain on the phone. By any chance could you come to Beatrice's home now for a few minutes so that I can show you the discrepancies and get your opinion. Beatrice will fully compensate you for your time."

"Yes, I can pop over now. I'll leave immediately and should arrive in about ten minutes."

"Thank you so much, Mr. Corbett. I look forward to meeting you. Goodbye."

"Who was that?" Astrid inquired.

"It was Beatrice's accountant. He's at her home now and needs to show me something about her legal account that he can't reconcile somehow."

"What do you think that could be?"

"It's strange. He said that he already called Belinda Cartright who suggested that he contact me. I can't imagine what it could possibly be about. Belinda has the actual file."

"Why couldn't he simply ask you over the phone?"

"He explained that it was too complex. I'm going to call Belinda at her office."

I called the main Kaufmann office number but just got the answering machine message saying that the office was closed.

Then I called Belinda's direct line but the call went directly to voice mail.

"It's possible I guess that Belinda could have been working a few minutes ago and has now gone home. I don't have her personal phone number."

I tried looking her up in the phone book but there was no residence listing. Many attorneys refused to publicize their home phone listings.

"Perhaps I'm being paranoid, Astrid, but would you call my smart phone in twenty minutes. If I don't answer, then call the police and send them to Beatrice's home. I'll write down her full address for you."

"If you do answer your phone but realize that you're in danger, how will I know if you can't actually tell me?"

"That's a good point. I've got an idea. If I sound calm and normal but call you Astridia, then you'll know that I'm in danger."

"I'm getting concerned, Jimmy."

"It's probably nothing but in the pit of my stomach what the accountant said didn't make a whole lot of sense. Given the fact that Beatrice was recently married to a con man, a bit of extra precaution seems prudent."

I left but I was determined to be on guard for any possible trouble.

By the time I arrived at Beatrice's huge home, I had

convinced myself that I was being silly.

I rang the front doorbell.

The door swung open and I walked inside only to discover Johnathan Jacobs brandishing a wicked looking handgun fitted with some sort of contraption on the barrel which I assumed to be a silencing device.

My gut instincts had been accurate.

CHAPTER 27 (Rebellious Lawyer)

Johnathan shut the door and barked at me to head upstairs.

When I entered the large bedroom, I was shocked to see Beatrice bound and gagged on the bed. At least she was alive.

Johnathan tossed me some plastic restraints and instructed me to place them on my ankles and then my wrists.

There was no point refusing since he was wielding the weapon.

Johnathan had me place myself in a sitting position on the bed with my bound wrists behind my neck. He then connected another restraint to secure my wrists to the bedpost behind me.

Next Johnathan pulled Beatrice up into a sitting position beside me and he yanked off the tape from her mouth.

My smart phone buzzed in my pants pocket.

Johnathan reached in and extracted the device.

"It's someone named Astrid Brownell," he muttered. "Who is that?"

"She's my new law partner."

"We don't need to answer. I won't tolerate interruptions to the business at hand."

"What is it that you want, Johnathan?"

"Beatrice seems to believe that you were solely responsible for penetrating my clever borrowed identity. I wanted to hear from your own lips before I blew your brains out just how you managed to discover than Johnathan Jacobs wasn't my real name."

Beatrice spoke for the first time since I'd arrived.

"I'm so sorry, Jimmy. Johnathan was just about to shoot me and I blurted out an insult that you were far more intelligent than Johnathan. That offended his little girl's ego and he decided to lure you here. It was never my intention to put you in harm's way."

"Get on with your explanation, Corbett. I haven't got all day."

For some strange reason my turd photographs from high school popped into my mind.

I had rebelled against the school forcing me to undertake a project I had no interest in.

Now this criminal was going to force me to grovel to his alleged superior intellect before he murdered both Beatrice and me.

I decided to go into full rebel mode.

"It's true, Arnold. You were completely outmatched by Team Corbett and Lantz."

Johnathan was taken aback.

"What did you just call me?"

"I used your former name, Arnold Kowalski. Now that I've met you, I can see that you don't have what it takes to be a Johnathan Jacobs. Arnold Kowalski accurately depicts you as a child of poverty-stricken immigrants. I bet you grew up within spitting distance of the train tracks in some big city slum."

"How did you discover my real name?"

"The police dusted your Toronto apartment for prints after you ran away from the lawsuit like a frightened child. Pathetic little Arnold didn't have the courage to stand and fight. You might actually have persuaded a judge that being married using a phony name was irrelevant to the fact that you cohabited with Beatrice for four years. We want to sincerely thank you for being such a pussy."

For a moment I feared that I'd gone too far with the insults but quickly reconsidered and decided that the aggressive response to this low-life was at least useful in keeping Beatrice and me alive hopefully long enough for help to arrive.

I sincerely hoped that the cops weren't dawdling at the donut shop before responding to Astrid's call that we needed immediate help.

"What else do you know about me?" Johnathan demanded.

Beatrice responded.

"We're aware that you spent three years in prison for financial scams."

I added that we had also learned that Arnold Kowalski had been charged with manslaughter and assault but had beaten the charges.

"Why don't you impress us now and tell us what mischief you've been up to between 2006 when you got out of prison and 2013 when you began using the Johnathan Jacobs alias?"

"I'd rather remain a man of mystery. I had intended to restart my life as Arnold Kowalski but now that I realize that the cops have married up Arnold and Johnathan, I'll have to utilize one of my other identities."

He paused for a moment before announcing that it was time for Beatrice and me to meet our maker.

"Don't you even want to know the details about how we outed you as a fraud?" I snarled.

"I don't think that will be necessary."

Johnathan raised the gun and pointed it at my face.

"I promised Beatrice that I'd force her to watch me plant a bullet in your brain before I killed her. Watch closely, love. This shyster's death is totally on you."

I interrupted.

"You were right, Beatrice. Johnathan's fragile ego won't allow him to absorb the details of how we crushed his pathetic plans. We'll have to visit him in his nightmares and taunt him with his total impotence. I can't wait to watch him piss his pajamas while he's dreaming."

My smart mouth certainly got Johnathan's attention.

He lifted his weapon above his head and brought it down on the left side of my cheek but his angle was wrong and I suffered only a glancing blow.

"Is that the best you've got, loser?" I taunted.

CHAPTER 28 (Last-Minute Rescue)

Johnathan raised his gun again, pointed it at my face and broke out in a truly evil grin.

"Die, shyster," he snarled as he began to pull the trigger.

At that precise moment my attention was diverted to the bedroom entrance.

Detective McCready was at the threshold with her own gun drawn.

"Drop the weapon," she shouted.

Johnathan had already committed himself to firing his own gun but the distraction affected his aim and his bullet whizzed past my face and blasted into the wall behind us. I felt a slight stinging in my left ear.

McCready fired off three rapid shots, each of which found its mark somewhere in Johnathan.

It was a gruesome sight. Beatrice screamed and I watched in horror as part of Johnathan's face was blown off.

I looked back at McCready who seemed to be in shock. She had just shot and killed a man.

"You saved our lives just in the nick of time, Anita. I felt Johnathan's bullet fly past my face."

"Your ear is bleeding," Beatrice blurted out. "Are you hurt, Jimmy?"

"My ear is stinging but I don't seem to be hurt."

McCready had her phone out and was calling for an ambulance and back-up.

When she had completed the call, I suggested that she take photographs immediately to show that we were tied up and at Johnathan's mercy.

The detective did as I advised and also took some pictures of Johnathan after she determined that he was well and truly dead.

"I'm so sorry but I don't have the equipment to remove the plastic restraints. I'll have my colleagues bring what we need. Your ear is bleeding, Jimmy. The

bullet must have grazed you. I
don't want to contaminate your
injury which doesn't seem serious.
The paramedics will tend to you
once they get here."

McCready called to request the
tools to remove the restraints and
then asked us to describe what had
occurred before she arrived on the
scene.

Beatrice handled the narrative.

Suddenly I realized that Astrid
must be worried sick so I
requested that McCready phone
Astrid and let her know that
Beatrice and I were fine and that
I'd fill her in on the details as
soon as I got home.

In fact it took more than two
hours before I was allowed to
leave Beatrice's house.

The paramedics arrived first and
they tended to my ear which had
only been slightly grazed by the
bullet. My cheek was also scraped
and sore from Johnathan's glancing
blow with the butt of his gun.

Finally police back-up showed up
and they cut away the plastic

restraints first on Beatrice and then the ones binding me.

Beatrice was immensely apologetic about endangering my life but I assured her that she had done the wise thing by stalling Johnathan.

The police interrogated McCready, Beatrice and me extensively before eventually telling me that I could go home.

Beatrice hugged me before I left. Her daughter was coming to drive Beatrice to the daughter's home to visit for a few days while the police completed any further investigation they required.

That time could also be utilized to expunge any and all evidence that Johnathan had been shot to death in the room.

I was surprisingly calm as I drove home.

CHAPTER 29 (Aftermath)

Astrid was horrified as I described the harrowing experience Beatrice and I had just been through.

"What would have happened if we hadn't made arrangements for me to call you?" she moaned.

"I'm afraid that it would have been my brains and Beatrice's splattered against the bedroom wall instead of a portion of Johnathan Jacobs' face. As it was, if Anita McCready hadn't distracted Johnathan as he was attempting to shoot me in the face, I'd also be dead although perhaps Beatrice would have been spared."

Astrid broke down in tears.

I attempted to console her with the truth, namely that I had survived the danger and that we had made an efficient team in anticipating that something was off with the accountant's phone call and taking precautionary measures.

The ensuing couple of weeks were quite interesting.

The local newspaper printed the story on the front page and portrayed me and Beatrice as brave hostages in the face of extreme danger.

Detective Anita McCready was awarded a citation for bravery.

The story as written was accurate and even I had to admit that the sequence of events was mesmerizing.

Everything had fallen completely into place to thwart Johnathan's wretched plans and bring harsh justice to bear on his depravity.

Beatrice invited Astrid and me for supper at her home on Saturday, March 27th. Detective McCready was also present as was Beatrice's daughter.

As we were finishing up dessert, Beatrice stood up and made an earthshattering announcement.

"Words can't convey my gratitude to Anita, Jimmy and Astrid for saving my life. As a small token of my appreciation, I want each of you to have a monetary reward."

Our collective jaws gaped open when we opened our individual envelopes to discover that Beatrice had enclosed a cheque to each of us in the amount of $500,000.

Beatrice assured us that these funds constituted just a small portion of her wealth and that the rewards had been fully earned.

Astrid and I used our rewards to purchase the small strip plaza where we had our office.

Anita McCready retired from the police force two days after receiving her money.

Another fortuitous result of the situation arose because of the newspaper article.

New clients began swarming into our law office and our future now seemed perfectly rosy.

Astrid and I fell even more deeply in love and planned to get married in the summer.

It had only taken a few months for the stubborn lawyer to exchange his life of lonely big city workaholic drudgery for a loving relationship and a rewarding career in a picturesque small town in rural Ontario.

Life couldn't get any better than that.

THE END

ABOUT THE AUTHOR

Donald W. Desaulniers is a retired lawyer who resides in the picturesque small city of Belleville, Ontario with his lovely British wife Jane and their cat Charlie.

Donald is a graduate of University of Waterloo (1968) and University of Western Ontario Law School (1971) and operated his own legal practice in Belleville from 1973 until he retired in 2009.

Donald took up writing fiction shortly after he retired. Always a proponent of quantity over quality, Donald has penned more than 100 novels since leaving the practice of law.

All of his books are available exclusively through Amazon as E-Books and as Paperbacks.

OTHER BOOKS BY THIS AUTHOR

SLIMY LAWYER SERIES

SLIMY LAWYER (#1 in Series)

SLIMY SUES AMERICA (#2 in Series)
SLIMY GETS SHAFTED (#3 in Series)
SLIMY GETS DISBARRED (#4 in Series)
SLIMY TASTES THE GOOD LIFE (#5 in Series)
SLIMY LAWYER CHECKS OUT (#6 in Series)

VANISHING LAWYER SERIES

VANISHING LAWYER (A World Without Me)
VANISHING LAWYER #2 (Unwanted Witness)
VANISHING LAWYER #3 (Fugitive Alien)
VANISHING LAWYER #4 (Saving the President)
VANISHING LAWYER #5 (Swindling Seniors)
VANISHING LAWYER #6 (Saving Trump Again)

WEIRD LAWYER SERIES

WEIRD LAWYER #1 (Novice Attorney)
WEIRD LAWYER #2 (Tough Times)
WEIRD LAWYER #3 (A Pinch of Jealousy)

OTHER LAWYER NOVELS

THE WRONG LAWYER (#1 in Series)
SNARKY LAWYERS (#2 in Series)

CARJACKED LAWYER (A Travel Nightmare)
LAWYER HEAVEN
THE LAWYER AND THE PRINCESS (A Love Story)
REVILED LAWYER
STUBBORN LAWYER (A Canadian Mystery)
DISCARDED LAWYER (But Not Dead Yet)
THE LAWYER WHO HATED MONEY
FEISTY OLD LAWYERS (Biting Bureaucracy)
LOCKDOWN LAWYER
SHUT THAT LAWYER UP
DIE NOW OLD MAN
PARADE OF DEAD LAWYERS
LUCKY LAWYER

RICH LAWYER, POOR PRIEST
THE LORD SNATCHES AWAY
LOATHING THE LAWYER, LOVING THE LAWYER
LADY LUCK LOVES LAWYERS
THE CHRISTMAS LAWYER
THE LAWYER'S MUSLIM NEIGHBORS
TERRORIST LAWYER
THE TWIN SHADOWS
REVENGE DELAYED
LAWYER IN THE TOILET
BUYING REDEMPTION
NAÏVE LAWYER
FAKE LAWYER

NOVELS WITH ROMANTIC THEMES

JOBLESS CHRISTMAS (A Travel Romance)
THE LAWYER AND THE PRINCESS (A Love Story)
BEVY OF BEAUTIES (Finding Love After Loss)
SWEET ROMANCE BACK HOME
LOVE SAVES A LONER
THE LIPPY LAWYER'S ROMANCE
THE CHEAPSKATE TWINS
BROKE, DISGRACED AND ALONE (A Romance)
A RETIRED LAWYER'S DOOMED ROMANCE
LOVE SEDUCES A FOOL

UNDERCOVER HILLBILLY ACTION/MYSTERY SERIES

UNDERCOVER HILLBILLY #1 (A Financial Mystery)
UNDERCOVER HILLBILLY #2 (Murder Suspect)
UNDERCOVER HILLBILLY #3 (A Stinking Mystery)
UNDERCOVER HILLBILLY #4 (Another Strange
Mystery)
UNDERCOVER HILLBILLY #5 (Missing Half-Brother)
UNDERCOVER HILLBILLY #6 (Dangerous Adversary)

TY WARD ADVENTURE SERIES

TY WARD HITS AMERICA (#1 in Series)
TY WARD'S HOLIDAY FROM HELL (#2 in Series)
TY WARD'S NEXT WAR (#3 in Series)
DEADLY WITNESS (#4 in Series)
A YOUNG HOOKER'S THANKS (#5 in Series)
TY WARD'S LAST WAR (#6 in Series)
TY WARD'S SHATTERED PEACE (#7 in Series)
TY WARD'S ROUGH JUSTICE (#8 in Series)
TY WARD'S LOCKDOWN RESCUE (#9 in Series)

OTHER ACTION NOVELS

ELUSIVE WITNESS (Hard to Kill)
STARTING OVER (Danger in Missouri)
CARJACKED LAWYER (A Travel Nightmare)
LADY INJUSTICE (Falsely Accused)
UNQUALIFIED DETECTIVE (A Financial Mystery)
TRAILER PARK REVENGE (Crime Thriller)
CROSSING A RICH MAN (Turning the Tables)
THE LEFT TACKLE'S CHRISTMAS
FIFTY YEARS LATER (Hitchhiking in Donald
Trump's America)
ESCAPE FROM EVERYTHING
MARTY MARCOTTE'S REVOLVING LIFE
VILE FAMILIES

WARD JONES #1 (Fledgling Predator)
WARD JONES #2 (Damsels in Distress)

SCIENCE FICTION/SUPERNATURAL NOVELS

FAILED LAWYER, POMPOUS ANGEL
TEMPTING THE GOOD LAWYER
ALIEN SPECTATORS
DIVERGENT LAWYER

YOUNG ADULT NOVELS

MYSTERY OF THE OLD DESK

YOUNG BUT NOT STUPID
CELESTIAL COINCIDENCE

NOVELS WRITTEN UNDER PEN NAME "LANCE MAJESTIK"

COLD CASE LAWYER
UNVACCINATED OLD LAWYER (Rebel Without a Jab)
BETTER TIMES (A Comeback Story)
OLD MIND YOUNG BODY (Body Switch)
LOVE IN OLEAN (An American Romance)
UNDERCOVER TRUCKER (An American Mystery)
CRAZY OLD LAWYER (A Talking Skin Tag)
LOVE MOCKS A LIMP DICK (War of the Sexes)

NOVELS WRITTEN UNDER PEN NAME "DURWARD GARBAGE"

TRIPLE GARBAGE (Three Short Novels)
WRONG PLACE, WORST TIME
ABANDONED ALIEN (Space Aliens for Donald Trump)
GOLDEN CHAOS (Stock Market Meltdown)
NASTY MAN (Mr. Jerk)
ALMOST A LAWYER
SQUANDERING MY FORTUNE
REVENGE FROM HER GRAVE
LAWYER ON THE RUN (Panhandling Attorney)
SCORNFUL FAMILY (Eating Insults)